Addie McCormick

AND THE STOLEN STATUE

Leanne Lucas

HARVEST HOUSE PUBLISHERS
Eugene, Oregon 97402

ADDIE MCCORMICK AND THE STOLEN STATUE

Copyright © 1993 by Leanne Lucas
Published by Harvest House Publishers
Eugene, Oregon 97402

Library of Congress Cataloging-in-Publication Data

Lucas, Leanne, 1955–
    Addie McCormick and the stolen statue / Leanne Lucas.
      p.   cm. — (Addie McCormick adventures ; bk. #3)
    Summary: Prayer helps heal the broken friendship between Addie and
Brian and their pal Nick, in time for the threesome to investigate the
mystery of a missing statue.
    ISBN 1-56507-080-1
    [1. Mystery and detective stories.   2. Friendship—Fiction.   3. Chris-
tian life—Fiction.]   I. Title.   II. Title: Addie McCormick and the stolen
statue.   III. Series: Lucas, Leanne, 1955-   Addie adventure series ; bk. 3.
PZ7.L96963Add   1993
[Fic]—dc20   92-25919
                                                                          CIP
                                                                          AC

Printed in the United States of America.

CHAPTER 1

Spies for Sale

"Today's the day," Nick whispered in Addie's ear. The two friends watched silently as Brian finished connecting the new VCR to the new television Miss T. had purchased earlier in the week. A videocassette of the movie *Spies for Sale* lay on the floor next to Brian.

Addie nodded and took a deep breath. She rubbed her arms vigorously, trying to warm up in the chilly house. It was early fall and the sun was moving in and out of grey clouds. It was a perfect day to watch old movies. But was it the right time to tell Brian their secret?

"That's all there is to it," Brian said and stepped back from the television with a satisfied smile. "This is a nice model," he commented as he studied the controls of the VCR. "Does Miss T. always buy expensive stuff?"

"She does now," Nick muttered and Addie gave him a warning look.

"She likes to know what she buys is going to last," Addie said. "Are we ready to start the movie?"

"Yep," Brian answered. "Where's Miss T.?"

"Here I am." The older woman entered the room, buttoning her sweater, then shaking her head and brushing her hand across the grey hair she kept pulled back in a bun. "I had to go downstairs and give that old furnace a kick to get it started."

Brian raised an eyebrow and Miss T. smiled. "Not really," she admitted. "It's a little more technical than that. Well, let's watch our movie."

Brian picked up a small remote control and knelt by Miss T.'s chair. "This control is for your VCR," he explained. "This button is fast forward, here's rewind, and record. These buttons determine what speed you record at—standard play, long play, or extended play. This one—"

Miss T. placed a gentle hand over his mouth and he stopped abruptly. "Just turn it on, dear," she said. "I'll learn all that later." Brian grinned and hit the play button.

Nick laughed as the VCR clicked and the movie credits rolled across the screen. "No, you won't," he said knowingly to Miss T. "We've had our VCR for years and my mom still can't figure it out. I have to program it whenever she wants to record a show."

"Well, I'm glad to know you're good for something," Miss T. retorted. Addie and Brian both laughed as Nick made a face at his elderly friend.

Addie settled comfortably on the old sofa and only half-listened as the friendly banter continued between the two. Her mind skipped back over the events of the past few months and she studied her friends gathered in front of the television.

Brian Dennison was the most recent addition to their small group. Nick's and Brian's parents had been friends for many years. Brian's mother had died two years ago and his father traveled extensively for a large restaurant chain, so Brian was spending the first semester of school with Nick and his family.

Addie had been wary of Brian at first, afraid that his friendship with Nick would not leave room for her. But the Lord had a way of working things out, and as usual, He'd worked it out better than she could have imagined.

Addie was a Christian and so was Brian. Although she knew from the start there was something different about him, that news had been quite a shock for Nick. Nick had always teased her about being a "religious nut." Discovering Brian was a nut too was almost more than he could handle. But Brian was a good friend, and his quiet witness paid off. By the end of the summer Nick had accepted the Lord as well. Addie learned then that God knew what He was doing, even if she didn't. Brian had been the answer to Addie's prayers for Nick.

Nick Brady was probably the best friend she had, even if he was a boy. He was her closest neighbor and the first person she met after moving here. Addie and Nick were alike in many ways—impulsive, fun-loving, and sometimes quick-tempered. Addie's mom thought their guardian angels must put in a lot of overtime, keeping them both out of trouble when they were together.

And it was together they had met Miss T., their elderly neighbor. Miss T. was a gruff but kind old woman who enjoyed the company of children. But Miss T. was poor and in danger of losing her home, until Addie and Nick made some exciting discoveries. A hidden room with valuable "antiques" and Miss T.'s secret past had all made for an exciting summer. Best of all, Miss T. never had to worry about money again.

When Brian joined them at the beginning of school, Miss T. asked that Nick and Addie keep her past a secret. The children agreed, and so far Addie thought they had done an admirable job of keeping their mouths shut. But it was difficult, especially when Brian proved to be such a trustworthy friend. Fortunately, Miss T. recognized that as well, and after much discussion with Addie's parents (who were also in on the secret) it was decided that Brian could, and should, be trusted with the news of Miss T.'s past.

And so they were gathered today to watch *Spies for Sale*. Addie shivered, partly from cold, but mostly from excitement. How would Brian react?

The names *Tierny Bryce* and *Winston Rinehart* filled the screen, written in longhand, the way many old movies presented their credits. Nick glanced at Addie and grinned. She grinned back, but shook her head and gave a slight nod toward Brian.

The movie was one of Addie's favorites. It was the story of a young soldier sent abroad during World War I to spy for his country. Halfway through the movie he was suspected of being a double agent. Of course, his girlfriend never doubted him for a minute, and she waited patiently for his return from the war.

While in Europe, the soldier was always being sent on the most dangerous assignments. He would mail his girl a statue after a mission was over. It was his way of telling her he was all right. The first statue showed a young man in uniform, standing erect with the United States flag over his shoulder. The second was of a soldier leaning on his gun. Soon the young woman had a beautiful collection.

The last statue, a soldier smiling, waving his hat in triumph, came special delivery to the heroine the day she learned of her fiancé's death. Shot and killed in the line of duty, his character was cleared of all suspicions and proclaimed a hero.

As the bereaved young woman's face filled the screen in the final scene, her bright blue eyes looked straight into the camera and Addie shivered again. Although many years had passed, those bright blue eyes had never changed.

The camera panned over the collection of statues, then the picture faded and the final credits began to roll. The room was silent for a long moment. Finally Miss T. spoke.

"So?" she asked briskly. "What did you think?"

Brian spoke first. "It was kinda corny, but the plot was good."

"Yeah," Nick said with some disgust. "Why do they have to ruin a perfectly good war story with all that romantic junk?"

"I thought it was touching," Addie said. She had been close to tears at the news of the young soldier's death. She was glad Nick hadn't seen her wipe her eyes. She never would have heard the end of it!

"His girlfriend didn't seem to be very shook up," Brian said nonchalantly. "She didn't even cry when she found out he was dead."

"That's because she was trying to be brave!" Addie exclaimed. She cast a quick glance at Miss T. The old woman was frowning at Brian.

"Forget brave," he said. His dark brown eyes twinkled merrily as he finally looked at Miss T. and smiled. "Next time," he told his elderly friend, "try a few tears. It gets 'em every time."

CHAPTER 2

Tierny Bryce

Miss T. didn't miss a beat. She gave a loud *humph* and shook her head.

"Next time? There isn't likely to *be* a next time," she said firmly.

Nick blushed his customary shade of red. "How did you figure it out?" he sputtered. "Addie and I never said a word!"

"*Addie* never said a word," Brian corrected. "You've let a lot of things slip. Nothing very important," he hastened to add when Miss T. fixed her glare on Nick. "Addie always stopped him before he could give away too much. She'd do one of these." Brian proceeded to frown, shake his head, and give a slight nod toward an imaginary person.

Nick laughed loudly and it was Addie's turn to blush. "I never realized you saw me do that," she said sheepishly. "And I can't believe you knew Miss T. was Tierny Bryce and never said anything!"

"Oh, I didn't know *who* she was until today," Brian assured his friend. "I just knew she had to be somebody."

"So what gave it away?" Nick asked.

"Did you recognize Miss T.'s baby blue eyes?" Addie said with an ornery grin at the elderly woman.

"Nope," Brian answered. "I thought I'd seen the actress before, but I didn't know she was Miss T. It wasn't until I saw that statue that everything finally clicked."

"What statue?" Addie and Nick chorused. Miss T. was smiling.

"You are much too observant, Mr. Dennison," she told Brian.

"*What* statue?" Nick repeated.

Brian looked at Miss T. and remained silent. Miss T. stood and walked over to the large walnut china closet that graced the east wall of the room.

"This statue," she said, opening the curved glass door and reaching carefully to the back of the cabinet. She eased the soldier waving his hat over the collection of old-fashioned shaving mugs and cradled it gently in her hands. Addie jumped up to examine the treasure and Nick followed.

"What's this?" Addie asked, turning the statue over. The letters KR were imprinted on the bottom.

"Probably the initials of the sculptor," Miss T. said. "These statues are all originals—made especially for *Spies for Sale*."

"I thought you sold everything to Russ," Nick exclaimed.

"Not everything," Miss T. admitted. "*Spies for Sale* was my favorite movie. I decided I couldn't part with everything, so I kept this statue back."

Brian raised his hand. "Time out. Who's Russ and what is 'everything'?"

"Russ is the man who helped Miss T. sell—" Addie began.

"'Everything' is all the old movie props Miss T. kept—" Nick interrupted.

Miss T. clapped her hands sharply and the two children stopped. "Since it's my story, why don't I tell it?" she asked.

Nick heaved a frustrated sigh but Addie nodded. "That's fair," she said.

"Thank you." Miss T. took a deep breath and began.

"Tierny Bryce was my stage name 45 years ago. Winston Rinehart was my co-star and Rinehart and Bryce became a fairly well-known couple. We made several movies together. *Spies for Sale* was one of the most popular.

"But I hated the Hollywood life. Too much pretense, no privacy. I became increasingly unhappy, especially when the movie studio insisted Winston and I fabricate a 'romance.'

"One night I was particularly upset about the way my life was going, and I drove my car home at a highly illegal speed. I slid through a curve, down a drop-off, and into a lake. I wasn't hurt and I managed to get out of the car safely, but it occurred to me I had a perfect way out of the Hollywood life.

"A friend helped me get out of town early the next morning. The body of 'Tierny Bryce' was never found in that lake, and I moved to this house with my sister. I've lived here in peace for 45 years.

"Then these two," here she arched an eyebrow at Addie and Nick, "started snooping around and discovered my secret. Since my funds were running low, they convinced me to sell the props I kept from my movie career. A man named Russ Krueger sold them to a museum in New York for a tidy sum, which has enabled me to remain in my home and live comfortably."

Brian glanced around him at the well-furnished room. "That explains a lot—including Amy," he said. Amy was Miss T.'s hired companion.

Nick was shaking his head and frowning. "It was a lot more exciting than that when it happened. You left out most of the important stuff, like how we met Russ in the first place and finding the secret room and meeting Winston Rinehart and—"

"What secret room?" Brian interrupted. "You *met* Winston Rinehart?"

Addie grinned and nodded. "It was great! We've been dying to tell you, but we knew we had to wait until Miss T. was ready."

Brian gave Miss T. a shy smile. "Thanks," he said simply.

Miss T. *humphed* again and patted his shoulder. "You have continually proven yourself to be a trustworthy boy, Mr. Dennison. I'm glad you know."

That was quite a compliment coming from Miss T., and no one knew what to say. Brian broke the embarrassed silence with a cough.

"Uh, what secret room?" he repeated.

Miss T. laughed. "Oh, that dirty, dirty room. I haven't been up there since the day Mr. Krueger carried everything down to be sold, and I didn't clean up then."

"We don't care," Nick said. "Can we show Brian the room?"

"Pleeeeease?" Addie begged.

"Of course," Miss T. smiled. "I've nothing to hide now." She reached for the remote control to the VCR and pressed the rewind button. "And I *will* learn how to program this contraption, Mr. Brady. Just see if I don't."

Nick rolled his eyes. "Anybody can push the rewind button," he muttered.

Miss T. rapped him gently on the head with the remote. "I'm not just anybody," she said. "Go on, now, find your secret room. I'm going to start supper. Amy's been busy raking leaves all afternoon. She'll be tired."

Addie led the way out of the room and began running down the hall after they were out of Miss T.'s sight. She and Nick raced for the attic door and the three children clamored noisily up two flights of stairs. Nick reached the attic first and threw open the heavy oak door.

The attic was even dirtier than the last time Nick and Addie had been there. Crops were being harvested and there was a fine layer of silky black dust over everything. Nick sneezed.

"This is dirty," Addie said.

The attic ran the length of the house and was almost empty, except for a few sacks and a trunk under one window. Brian looked around in disappointment.

"This isn't what I expected," was his only comment.

"Of course it's not," Nick said. "This isn't the secret room."

Now Brian was confused. "It's not? Is there another level?" he asked, looking around for more stairs.

"Nope." Addie and Nick both watched their friend, waiting to see if he would be able to figure out the mystery. He didn't disappoint them.

"Then there has to be a secret entrance," he said with excitement and began searching the walls and the floor for a hidden door or passage. Several minutes later he was covered with dust, but not ready to admit defeat.

"Okay, give me a clue," he finally said.

"What's wrong with the attic?" Addie asked. "What's missing?"

"How should I know?" he answered. "I've never been up here—" He stopped and his eyes grew wide as he stared intently at the west wall. Then he glanced behind him and to both sides. Finally he grinned. "There's supposed to be a window right there," he said, pointing at the solid wall.

Addie nodded, and Brian began searching the wall with renewed vigor. He found the telltale crack quickly and began pushing, then pulling, and finally scratching the wall with his fingernails.

Nick laughed at the fevered impatience of his usually docile friend. "I can never get it open, either. Addie has to do it."

Brian gave up and stepped back. Addie pressed gently on the hidden spring. The door popped back at her touch and she slipped her fingers into the small crack that appeared. There was a loud creak as she slid the door open and stepped to one side to let Brian in.

The smile of delight on his face faded to a look of pure astonishment. Nick's eyes practically popped out of their sockets and Addie felt goosebumps race up her arms. What was the matter? She spun around and peered quickly over Brian's shoulder. The sight she saw took her breath away.

CHAPTER 3

Unusual Guests

Addie found herself staring into a masked face. There was a startled, sleepy look in the big brown eyes, and Addie gasped with delight as the raccoon sat up and rubbed its nose with its front paw. Four more raccoons stirred inside a chewed-up cardboard box.

"Don't move too fast or you'll scare them," Brian whispered. Even that warning was enough to rouse the racoons to action. The one on the bottom pushed his way to the top, tumbling two others out of the box and onto the floor close to the feet of the children. Addie squealed and stepped back but Nick reached out to touch one. Without warning the largest racoon growled and rose from the box with a speed that surprised all three children.

"Holy cow!" Nick yelled and pushed Brian out the door. Addie had already made a hasty retreat and stood waiting to pull the panel shut behind them. They stood there gasping for breath, and then burst into relieved laughter.

"How did they get in there?" Addie finally managed to ask.

"Who knows?" Nick shrugged. "There must be a hole in the roof somewhere."

Brian nodded. "Could be. Let's take another look and see if they've left."

Addie had not closed the panel completely and Brian put his fingers in the narrow slit and opened the panel another inch. He peered into the secret room, then opened the panel farther and pointed silently . Between the rafters and the roof, the children could see the bushy ringed tail of the last raccoon disappearing through a dark hole.

"The big one that growled was the mother," Brian said.

"They were all big," Addie exclaimed.

Brian nodded. "They're putting on a lot of fat and their fur is getting thicker. They're getting ready for winter."

"How do you know that wasn't the father?" Nick asked. "It was huge! Too big to be a female."

Brian shook his head. "The father never sticks around. The female takes all the responsibility for the kits after they're born."

"Those were babies?" Addie was incredulous.

"Well, baby is kind of a relative term," Brian grinned. "They're her children and she was ready to protect them, but I think they could probably have protected themselves."

The children stepped back into the room and began to look around. Although all the movie props had been removed, there were still boxes, bags, and hangers scattered around the room. Crumpled up newspaper that was once packing for Miss T.'s treasures had been ripped to shreds. Corn cobs littered the room and kernels of corn were everywhere.

"They certainly made themselves at home," Nick commented. "What a mess."

"Let's go tell Miss T.," Addie suggested.

The three children clattered down the stairs and tumbled into the kitchen. Miss T. was at the sink and she turned with a frown at the noise.

"You sounded like a troop of elephants coming down those stairs!" she exclaimed. "What on earth is the matter?"

"Raccoons!" Nick announced. "You've got a whole family living in your attic."

Amy entered the kitchen from the back porch and heard Nick's proclamation. She nodded her head in confirmation. "I just saw them coming down the big sugar maple next to the house," she said. "A mother and four kits—big ones!"

Miss T. dried her hands on a dish towel. "So the rascals finally made it into the house. I've never had *that* happen."

"Have you had other problems?" Brian asked.

"Oh, yes," Miss T. said. "Raccoons have tipped over my garbage can every year for the last 45 years."

"Why don't you just put your garbage can in the greenhouse?" Brian asked with a puzzled look.

Miss T. smiled and winked. "I kind of like the little boogers," she admitted and all three children laughed. So did Amy. "They're a lot of fun to watch. But I never get too close," she warned. "They'll bite if they feel threatened."

Nick grinned sheepishly. "Yeah, we got that idea."

Everyone trooped back to the attic, and Miss T. surveyed the damage. "Well, it's not as bad as it could be." She frowned. "I don't understand why they never got in before, though."

Amy snapped her fingers. "The roofers haven't put the soffits on this side of the house yet."

Miss T. nodded. "We'll call them Monday. We'll clean up the mess after they get them up. That way we won't have to do it twice, in case our friends come back tonight."

An idea had been forming in Addie's mind. She spoke quickly, before she lost her nerve. "We'll be glad to help you clean, Miss T." She saw Nick mouth a silent *Oh, we will?* behind the older woman, but she ignored him. "Do you think we could use the room as a secret club when we're finished?"

Nick's eyes widened in surprise and Brian grinned. Miss T. and Amy exchanged an amused glance.

"Frankly, dear," said Miss T., "I'm surprised you haven't asked before. I've always thought this room would make a wonderful place to play."

"All right!" Nick exclaimed.

"Thanks, Miss T.," Brian said.

"We'll clean next week, after the soffits are up," said Miss T. "I might even spring for some paint, if you want to do it up right. And I'll call the heating and plumbing man and have him connect the heating duct to this section of the attic. I had them all removed years ago, but if you plan to be up here much, you'll need some heat."

"Is there any electricity?" Brian asked.

"What color paint?" Addie wanted to know.

"Can we bring up some furniture?" Nick chimed in.

"Yes. It's up to you. And yes." Miss T. answered their questions in quick succession. "Now, I've got to finish supper." She stepped out of the room and Amy followed her. "Talk over what you want to do," she threw over her shoulder, "and I'll order the paint Monday morning."

They watched the older women disappear down the attic steps, then all three children began talking at once.

"Blue! It's got to be blue. I love blue—"

"I've got tons of posters my mom won't let me put up. We could cover one wall with the Chicago Bears—"

"This will be a perfect place to put my computer. Your mom won't let me keep it out because of Jesse Kate—"

Just as suddenly, they stopped and looked at one another. Then Addie spoke.

"I do *not* want Chicago Bears posters everywhere!"

"Well, I don't want blue walls!"

Addie and Nick glared at one another and Brian raised his hand. "Do we at least agree on my computer?" he asked.

"We'll talk about it," Nick grumbled, still glaring at Addie. "We won't be able to do much next week, anyway," he said. "I've got football practice every night after school."

"So?" Addie asked.

"You can't come without me!" Nick protested.

Addie and Brian exchanged a glance. "Well, Nick," Brian began.

"I said you can't!" Nick stood with his arms crossed, feet spread. He looked ready to fight.

"Why not?" Addie asked crossly. "Life doesn't stop just because you've got football practice."

"It wouldn't be fair!"

Brian spoke. "It will take us an awfully long time if we only work on Saturdays," he said reasonably.

"But . . . I . . . You can't—" Nick searched in vain for a legitimate protest and finally gave up. "All right," he snapped. "Go ahead without me. Paint the stupid room blue and set up your computer. I don't care." He turned and stormed out of the room and down the stairs.

CHAPTER 4

Food Fight!

Addie and Brian listened in silence as Nick's angry footsteps faded away. Far below them they heard the faint slam of the screen door.

Addie stooped over to pick up a crumpled paper bag. She opened it with a snap and began picking up corn cobs and dropping them into the bag. The dust tickled her nose and she sneezed. Brian walked over to the west window and gazed out at the farmland below.

"What do we do now?" he asked quietly.

Addie sighed. "I don't know. I wish Nick had never decided to play football."

Brian nodded. "He doesn't even like football that much."

Addie kicked first one corn cob, then a second, then a third across the dusty floor. "I just don't understand him sometimes! Why does he think he has to be right in the middle of everything that goes on? Did he tell you he wants to try out for the school play next week? And he's talking about joining the Science Club, too."

"I think being in a new school is really hard for Nick," Brian said. "You and I are used to moving around, but Nick isn't. He's never been on the 'outside' before. Getting involved in different things is his way of feeling like he's part of a group."

"Why does he have to be part of any group?" Addie grumbled. "He's already part of ours."

Brian shrugged. "I guess that's not enough." He paused. "Besides, I'd kind of like to join the Science Club myself."

Addie smiled faintly. "I know. I thought about trying out for the school play." The smile faded. "But I'm trying out because I like drama. And you're joining the Science Club because you like science. We're not trying to—to impress people."

"I'm not sure Nick even knows he's trying to impress people, Addie. He's just trying to fit in the best way he knows how."

Addie shook her head. "Have you noticed how some of the guys on the football team act? I don't think it's a good idea for him to fit in with *that* group."

"Probably not," Brian agreed. "But you've got Christian parents who point out those things to you. And my dad always taught me to be my own person and not just follow the crowd. Nick's parents don't seem to worry about that kind of stuff."

"You can say that again!" Although Nick was a new Christian, his parents were not. The memory of Mr. Brady's reaction to Nick's new-found faith was still fresh in Addie's mind.

"You did what?" his father bellowed.

"I accepted Christ," Nick repeated softly.

"What's that mean?" Mr. Brady asked Mrs. Brady. "What's that mean?" he asked his son. "You were baptized years ago. What else do you need?"

"Now, dear," Mrs. Brady interrupted, "I think it just means that Nick understands the importance of—of, well, you know."

"No, I don't know," his father bellowed again. "What do you understand now that you didn't understand before?"

Nick swallowed hard. "Aw, Dad—"

"No, I mean it," Mr. Brady insisted. "What does this 'accepting Christ' mean?"

Nick took a deep breath. "It means that I—I know that my sins are forgiven because Jesus died for them and—and now I want to obey God and—and pray," Nick finished triumphantly.

Addie was impressed. For a rookie Christian, that was a pretty good explanation.

"Obey *God*?" his father questioned.

Now Brian spoke up. "Oh, God always wants you to obey your parents, too," he said helpfully. "He hardly ever asks you to do something your . . . parents . . . don't . . . like." He trailed to a stop.

"Hardly ever?"

Now it was Brian's turn to swallow. "Hardly. Ever."

Mr. Brady arched an eyebrow at his wife. "I told you that church was going to put weird ideas in their heads," he muttered. To Nick he said, "Okay. Obey God if you want to, but obey me regardless. And pray if you want to. Just don't let anybody catch you doing it."

"Addie?" Amy stood just outside the door of the secret room and her soft voice interrupted Addie's reverie. "Is everything all right?"

Addie shook her head and Amy sighed. "I was afraid not," the woman said. "Nick seemed very angry when he left."

"Nick's in football and he doesn't want us to come here without him on the days he has football practice," Brian informed her.

Amy frowned. "How often does he have practice?"

"Every day," Addie said. "He doesn't even like football that much. He only joined because he thought it would make everyone notice him."

Amy nodded. "I see. Then we need to pray and ask the Lord to show us how we can help Nick."

Addie and Brian exchanged a sheepish glance, then closed their eyes while Amy prayed. "Lord, we know Nick is having a difficult time adjusting to a new school. I ask that You give Addie and Brian the wisdom they need to help him through this difficult time. Make them sensitive to Nick's feelings and help them reach a solution to this problem that will satisfy everyone. Thank You, Lord. In Jesus' name, Amen."

"Amen," Brian echoed softly.

"Amen," Addie said reluctantly. She wanted to be sensitive to Nick's needs, but what about her needs, and Brian's? She hoped God didn't expect them to do everything Nick wanted just because he was a baby Christian.

Brian and Addie closed the door to the secret room and left Miss T.'s. When they turned the corner to Nick's house, they could see him waiting for them, riding circles in the road. They approached him in silence and he greeted them with a rueful smile.

"I'm sorry," he said immediately. "I guess I'm being pretty selfish. I shouldn't keep you from going to Miss T.'s just because I can't. That's just one of the consequences I'll have to pay for being in football. Coach says you've got to be willing to make a lot of sacrifices if you want to be a good player."

Addie didn't think she wanted to be one of the sacrifices, but she didn't say so. Brian slapped his friend on the back.

"Thanks, Nick," he exclaimed. "Maybe you can come for a little while after practice every day. You're home by 4:30, aren't you?"

Nick nodded. "I can help for half-an-hour or so," he agreed. "At least until it starts getting dark early." He laughed suddenly. "I don't know why I should object to having you two do all the work!"

"I wondered how long it would take for you to think of that," Addie said wryly.

They talked briefly for a few more minutes, then Addie left for home and Nick and Brian went inside.

* * *

The next Monday at school Nick, Addie, and Brian sat down to lunch. Nick took a huge bite of his grilled cheese sandwich and began talking.

"So, you guyth goin' a Miss T.th's today?"

"Nick!" Addie exclaimed at the sight of chewed-up cheese.

"Wha?" he said with a laugh, and a gob of cheese fell out of his mouth and onto his plate. Several other kids laughed and Nick grinned, showing more bread and cheese. He chewed with his mouth open, slowly and deliberately.

Addie made a face and ignored him. Brian just rolled his eyes.

By this time, several other boys had joined in the "see food" display and there was a lot of laughter, gags, and gross remarks.

"Hey, Brady, swallow this!" Tony Knight, one of Nick's football buddies, threw a cold French fry at Nick and hit him on the side of the head.

"Cut it out, Knight!" Nick yelled and threw the fry back. Soon the air was thick with French fries and Addie grabbed her tray and ran for the door. Brian and several other kids were right behind her and they almost ran into Mr. Beland, the superintendent.

"All right!" Mr. Beland shouted. "Knight, Colby, Johnson, Acker, and—and you," he faltered, pointing at Nick. "In my office immediately, if not sooner!" He did an abrupt about-face and left a shocked and silent cafeteria.

The silence only lasted a few seconds. "Way to go, Knight," said Jared Acker. A final fry whizzed through the air past Tony's head.

"Brady started it," he retorted.

"Yeah, Brady," chimed in several voices and Jared began pummelling Nick's arm. The five boys made their way out of the cafeteria, feigning bravado and talking loudly. They passed Addie and Brian in the doorway, and Tony gave Addie a mocking smile.

"Addie, would you pray for us?" he pleaded in a dramatic voice and everyone within earshot laughed.

When Addie didn't answer, Tony went on. "Why don't you and Nick and Brian the Brain here have a prayer meeting? Ask God to deliver us from our sins!" He spoke in the fake, wavery voice used by some of the television evangelists, and there was more laughter and a chorus of "Amen's."

Now Tony was on a roll. He dropped to his knees and grabbed Nick's hand. "Puhleeze, Brother Brady, pray for me!"

Nick shook off his friend, but made a quick sign of the cross over his head and Tony shouted, "Oh, thank you, Brother Brady, I'm forgiven!"

Their laughter rang out all the way down the hall. Nick refused to turn and look at Addie and Brian, but his neck was as bright a red as Addie had ever seen.

Addie was so angry she could barely contain herself. "How could he do that?!" she fumed.

"Addie—" Brian began quietly.

"He's no different than they are." Addie spit the words out and this time Brian snapped back.

"Stop it, Addie." His tone surprised her and she pressed her lips together to keep from saying any more.

"Give him some slack," Brian continued in a milder voice. "We all do stupid things sometimes. Why should Nick be any different? Don't expect more of him than God does."

"Ohhhhh," she muttered in frustration and dumped her uneaten lunch in the trash. "You're just—just too forgiving!" She slammed her tray on the cart and left Brian standing in the door of the cafeteria. The hypocrisy of her own words rang in her ears, but she didn't care.

CHAPTER 5

"Is She Alive Today?"

Addie sat in the very last seat of the bus, her nose pressed against the dirty window. She stared out over the busy school parking lot and watched as Nick and half-a-dozen other boys piled into the grey van that would take them to the community center for football practice.

Someone dropped into the seat in front of her. Addie knew it was Brian, but she didn't look up. She watched the grey van until it disappeared down the street. Then the bus's engine roared to life, and they chugged slowly past the school and into the street. She finally sat up straight and looked at Brian. His troubled brown eyes were watching her anxiously.

"Are you going to ignore me all the way home?" he asked bluntly.

"Of course not," she sighed. "I'm sorry I've been so nasty today, Brian. I'm just confused. I wish Nick would start acting like his normal self again."

"Addie, launching his lunch *is* normal for Nick."

Addie laughed for the first time that day. "Oh, I know," she said. "I meant the way he's been acting around the other football players. Today in the cafeteria, I felt like he was almost ashamed of being my friend. When Tony started making fun of me for being a Christian, I thought Nick might stand up for me. But he didn't. He went along with them, Brian! He made fun of me, too."

Addie's voice broke and she turned her head and wiped an angry tear from her eye. "And he's supposed to be a Christian!"

"He *is* a Christian, Addie," Brian said firmly. "I still think you're expecting more from Nick than he can give right now. And don't tell me I'm being too forgiving," he warned when she began to sputter. "Tell that to God!"

Addie closed her eyes and muttered, "You're too forgiving, God." When she opened them, Brian was staring at her in wide-mouthed disbelief. She closed them hastily. "I'm sorry, Lord, I didn't mean that. Really, I didn't. I'm sorry."

Brian breathed a sigh of relief. Addie slumped down and propped both knees against the back of Brian's seat. She laid her head back against the worn leather and sighed, her eyes still closed. "I am sorry, Lord. Help *me* to be more forgiving."

"Peter denied Jesus three times, and God still forgave him," Brian reminded her.

"I know, I know," Addie said. "But I'm not God."

"And for that fact I will be eternally grateful," Brian intoned in a somber voice, and Addie kicked his seat.

"Do you think Nick will come out to Miss T.'s today?" she asked him.

Brian shook his head. "I talked to him after class. He and the other guys who were throwing French fries have to come back after football practice and serve a detention."

"Why *after* practice? Why not instead of practice?" Addie wanted to know.

"Because they serve their detention with the principal, Mr. Stayton, and Mr. Stayton is also the football coach."

"I think that's what my dad would call conflict of interest,'" Addie grumbled. Brian only laughed.

The bus turned the corner to Nick's house and Brian picked up his books and prepared to leave. "I'm hungry," he told Addie. "I want to eat something before we go to Miss T.'s."

"Me, too," she agreed. "I'll be back in about half-an-hour."

Forty minutes (and a sandwich, an apple, and two glasses of milk) later, Addie and Brian were on Miss T.'s back porch. Addie banged on the screen door, then opened it, and stepped into the kitchen. "Hi, Miss T.! Hi, Amy!" she called out. "It's me and Brian."

Miss T. appeared in the kitchen door with her customary frown on her face. "What colors did you decide on?" she asked in way of greeting.

Addie shrugged. "We didn't, really." She hesitated. "We couldn't agree."

Miss T. clucked her tongue. "So I heard. Well, then, I'll decide for you. Especially since Francine brought these cans of paint by today. I told her you were going to fix up the attic and she said you could use the paint they had left over from their boys' rooms if we wanted to save some money."

Addie tried not to grimace. She doubted that she and Francine had the same taste in colors. Francine was Miss T.'s niece and a kind woman, but she tended to whine and complain a lot.

"What colors are they?" Brian asked in a too-cheerful voice. Addie could tell he wasn't thrilled with the idea either, and he didn't even know Francine.

Of course, Miss T. knew the children too well not to recognize their hesitation and she laughed gruffly. "Oh, don't worry," she said. "If you absolutely hate these colors, we'll get different ones. I just thought it might be easier on your friendship if you didn't have to make the decision yourselves."

Neither Addie nor Brian could think of an answer to that, so they remained silent while Miss T. opened the cans.

"Here's a full can—well, almost full—of white. That could be your basic color. Then we've got this— I don't know, green? Turquoise?"

"Turquoise," Addie said.

"And some lavender." Miss T. showed the two children the last can.

Addie surveyed the colors with some surprise. "Did Francine pick these out?"

"Of course not," Miss T. said. "Her boys did. She would have picked out something much more sensible. Willard took them to get the paint. Just like him to let them get something wild."

Addie had never met Willard, but Miss T. never had anything good to say about him. Addie always wondered what kind of man could live with Francine. Looking at the turquoise and lavender paint, her opinion of Willard went up a notch.

"Do you think Nick will like these colors?" she asked Brian.

He nodded. "Haven't you seen his new jacket? It's a little bit darker green than that, and it's trimmed in purple."

"That's right!" Addie exclaimed. She smiled at Miss T. "These will be just great. We'll paint the walls white and then each of us can think up our own design and paint it on in turquoise and lavender."

"Good enough." Miss T. put the lids back on the cans of paint. "But that's for another day. Today, you clean." She stopped then and peered out the back door. "Where is Mr. Brady?"

Addie glanced at the clock. "Either finishing football practice or starting his detention."

"Detention? What did he get a detention for?"

"Throwing French fries at lunch," Brian answered.

Miss T. clucked her tongue again. "Well, I can't say much about that. Been in a food fight myself." With that unexpected revelation, she left the kitchen.

Addie and Brian exchanged surprised looks and followed her into the living room.

"When did *you* get in a food fight?" Addie demanded.

Miss T.'s eyes twinkled and she laughed. "Oh, it was so long ago. On the set of *The Lady Wore Red*. We were filming a very elegant party scene set at Buckingham Palace. But it was past time for lunch and we were all starved. The director didn't want to stop the shoot because we were behind schedule. But everyone was so grouchy from hunger he told us we could take half-an-hour and eat in our costumes.

"Well, the 'Queen of England' chose broccoli soup for her lunch and about halfway through the meal her crown slipped off and landed right in the middle of her bowl. Of course, it showered everyone near her with creamed broccoli. I'm not sure who made the next move, but it wasn't more than two seconds and food was flying everywhere."

Addie laughed with delight. "Did you throw anything?"

"What a question! Of course I did." Miss T. paused. "I discovered if you want to make a real mess, mashed potatoes are the best weapon. For distance, use baked potatoes."

She stopped suddenly and frowned at the two children. "However, school is *not* the appropriate place for a food fight."

"Where is?" Brian asked with a huge grin.

"*Humph.* Good point. Probably shouldn't have told you that story."

"Don't worry, Miss T.," Addie assured her. "If we ever have a food fight, we'll make sure it's in an 'appropriate' place!"

"Oh, hush," Miss T. said. She shooed them out of the living room and back to the kitchen. She gave Addie a box of plastic garbage bags and Brian the broom. "Go on, now. Start cleaning and forget about food fights."

Addie and Brian laughed and started up the attic stairs. Behind them, they could hear Miss T. muttering, "Probably going to regret telling *that* story."

Once in the attic, Addie opened the secret door and they stepped into the dusty room. They checked all the empty cardboard boxes, but there were no signs of raccoons, so they set to work.

Cleaning was simply a matter of picking up and throwing away everything that was left in the room. Brian smashed boxes by stepping on them and Addie picked up the rest of the corn cobs. After an hour they had three plastic garbage bags filled with debris. The room had darkened considerably and they decided to quit for the day.

"We'll have to sweep and wash everything down with soap and water tomorrow," Addie said on the way downstairs.

"Then we can start painting on Wednesday," Brian answered.

Miss T. and Amy were not in the kitchen so Addie stuck her head in the living room door. The two women were watching television.

"We're going home, Miss T. We got a lot done today—" Addie began, but the old woman interrupted her.

"Ssshhh!" she said with a wave of her hand.

Addie looked at Brian and shrugged. Then she heard the name "Tierny Bryce" mentioned on the news broadcast Miss T. was watching. She motioned to Brian and they both stepped into the living room.

The news reporter was a well-dressed, good-looking young woman. Her backdrop was the famous HOLLYWOOD sign on the hillside. But it was her words that riveted Addie and Brian to the screen.

"Although it has been more than a month since the sale of artifacts from the Rinehart and Bryce movies, the controversy has not died. Where did these artifacts come from? Winston Rinehart has not been able to give us a satisfactory answer.

"And that, of course, leads us to the inevitable and never-answered question. Did Tierny Bryce really die that fateful night 45 years ago? Her body was never found. If she *is* alive, where is she today?"

CHAPTER 6

Another Fight

There was more to the report, but Miss T. didn't hear any of it. She stared vacantly over the top of the television and blinked her eyes rapidly.

Addie knelt next to her elderly friend's chair and placed her hand gently on Miss T.'s arm. "It's okay, Miss T. They won't find you."

The girl's soft voice seemed to jar Miss T. back to reality, and the old woman gave a short, bitter laugh. "You don't understand the bulldog mentality of Hollywood. Once they get hold of a story, they don't let go."

"They let go 45 years ago," Brian reminded her. "They'll let go again. Just give them time."

"No." Miss T. shook her head sadly. "Now that those artifacts are on display, there will always be someone trying to find the answer to that question."

Addie swallowed hard. "I'm sorry, Miss T.," she whispered.

"Why?" Miss T. brushed Addie's long black hair away from her face. "Because I ran away 45 years ago? Don't be. It's not your fault things have taken the turn they have."

"But if Nick and I hadn't snooped into your private life—"

"If you and Mr. Brady hadn't snooped, I'd be practically penniless and in a nursing home," Miss

T. interrupted her. "What's worse, I would never have known you and your families."

"But now you might lose—"

"What? My privacy? There are worse things to lose." Miss T. stared back at the television and sighed. "If they find me, I will learn to live with it. What other choice is there?"

"Is that Winston Rinehart?" Brian asked suddenly. He pointed to the television.

Winston Rinehart filled the small screen and Addie couldn't help but smile at the sight of the dignified old gentleman. She had only met him once, but his kind smile and melodious voice were just the same.

Amy picked up the remote and turned up the volume.

"Suffice it to say, the artifacts from the Rinehart and Bryce movies have been in safekeeping for many years. You need not know more than that," Winston was saying.

"But *who* had them in safekeeping?" one reporter persisted. "And where?"

Winston merely smiled and shook his head. The door to his spacious New York home opened silently behind him and he stepped inside with a final wave to the group clustered behind a mass of wires, microphones, and camcorders.

"Now they're dragging Mr. Rinehart into it," Addie said glumly.

Miss T.'s laugh was genuine this time. "Winston *loves* publicity," she informed them. "He's having more fun than he's had in years. Don't worry about him."

There were several more shots of Winston Rine-hart leaving his home, leaving a restaurant, leaving the opera. Each time the actor was confronted with a microphone, he was gracious and charming.

"He's kind of a classy old guy, isn't he?" Brian asked.

"Very," Miss T. agreed with a smile. "I miss him."

The phone rang suddenly and shrilly, and every-one jumped. Amy and Miss T. exchanged a nervous glance. Then Miss T. frowned.

"Oh, this is silly," she exclaimed. "They're not camping on my doorstep yet. Hello?"

She listened briefly and nodded. "Yes, they're still here, John."

At the mention of her father's name, Addie sat up with a start and looked out the window. It was dark.

"All right," Miss T. continued. "It's really not their fault, John. We were just listening to a report on television about 'Tierny Bryce.'" She paused. "You saw it, too? No, I'm not worried. All right. We'll see you in a few minutes."

She hung up the phone. "Your father," she said to Addie. "He's coming to pick you up. We'll put your bikes in the greenhouse for the night. You can pick them up tomorrow. Mr. Dennison, you'll find the key for the greenhouse on the hook by the back door."

They all trooped out to the kitchen and Brian began to sift through the keys. "This one?" he held up a single key on a chain.

"No, no, that's the spare key to the house," Miss T. shook her head. "It's a smaller key, for a pad-lock."

"Got it." Brian took the key and went outside to put the bikes away.

"You want some help?" Addie called.

"No, I got it." Addie could see Brian expertly handling both bikes, taking them to the greenhouse.

Turning her attention back to the kitchen, Addie couldn't resist peeking in the cookie jar. She wasn't disappointed. Fresh chocolate chip cookies!

"Don't ruin your supper," Miss T. admonished.

"Nothing ruins my supper," Brian exclaimed as he reentered the kitchen and reached in the jar.

"Mine, either," said Addie. She grabbed two cookies. "One for my dad," she told Miss T., and the woman smiled. Addie had inherited her chocolate chip cookie addiction from her father.

Headlights from the road turned down Miss T.'s long driveway. Brian peered out the screen door and stopped dead in his tracks. Then he motioned to Addie.

"Sshhh," he whispered and pointed to the garbage can that sat halfway between the back porch and the greenhouse.

In the glare of the headlights, Addie could see the unnatural reddish glint of several pairs of eyes. The raccoons had returned and were attempting to open Miss T.'s garbage can.

Mr. McCormick must have seen the raccoons at the same time, because he tooted the horn softly and they scurried across the backyard and into the woods behind Miss T.'s house.

"They're getting braver," Miss T. remarked. She held open the screen door and Addie and Brian ran down the back steps and out to the waiting car.

"Bye, Miss T., bye, Amy," Addie called over her shoulder.

"See you tomorrow," Brian added.

The two women waved and Mr. McCormick backed down the drive and headed for home.

"Where's Nick?" he asked his daughter between bites of chocolate chip cookie.

"Probably still serving his detention," Addie responded.

"What for?"

"Throwing French fries at lunch."

Mr. McCormick remained quiet and in the dusk, Addie couldn't tell if the expression on his face was a smile or a frown.

"Don't tell me you've been in a food fight, too?!" she exclaimed.

"What makes you think that?" he laughed.

"Because we told Miss T. what happened to Nick and we found out about a food fight she was in," Brian said.

"Somehow, that doesn't surprise me." Mr. McCormick laughed again. "No, I can honestly tell you I've never been in a food fight," he said.

Addie relaxed.

"Your mother has," he said nonchalantly.

"What!" Addie exploded and Brian burst into laughter.

"I'm sure she'd be thrilled to tell you the story sometime." Mr. McCormick was grinning mischievously.

Addie could hardly believe it. Her own mother? The same woman who insisted you put your fried chicken bones and corn cobs on a clean plate and not on the table? Grown-ups. Addie would never understand them.

* * *

The next morning Brian and Nick boarded the bus and sat in front of Addie. Nick could hardly bring himself to look Addie in the eye.

"I'm sorry, Addie. About yesterday, I mean. I don't know why I acted that way."

His expression was so genuinely miserable, Addie forgave him immediately.

"That's okay, Nick," she assured him. "I know those guys can be pretty intimidating sometimes."

Nick only nodded and stared out the window.

"Was your dad upset about your detention?" she asked.

Nick rolled his eyes and looked at Brian. "What do you think, Brian? Was he upset?"

Brian nodded. "Just a little."

"Huh! A little. 'If you ever let those hoods get you in trouble again, you're off the team for good.'" Nick imitated his father's gruff voice perfectly.

Addie had secretly prayed that would be his reaction, but she didn't say so. Nick understood her silence, though, and frowned at her.

"You wouldn't care, would you? You don't think I should be on the team in the first place, do you?"

Addie didn't answer.

Nick began to sputter. "I know I wasn't a very good—good defender yesterday—"

"Witness," Addie corrected softly.

"Whatever," Nick said with a frown. "But it's hard when your friends make fun of what you believe."

"I know," Addie said. She wanted to remind Nick of all the times he had teased her about praying before he became a Christian, but she didn't. *Dad would be proud of me*, she thought. *I'm getting pretty good at holding my tongue.*

"I know you two don't like them, but if you got to know some of the guys on the football team, maybe you'd change your minds."

Addie shrugged. "How am *I* ever going to get to know the football team, Nick?"

"We could show Tony and Jared the secret room," he suggested.

"*Nick!* Did you tell them about—"

"No, no, no," Nick interrupted Addie hastily. "Of course not. I'd never do that without asking you guys first. Don't you trust me?"

Addie didn't answer and Nick glared at her. "Why can't I invite some of my other friends to Miss T.'s?" he fumed.

"Because, Nick!"

"Because why? Don't tell me you haven't thought of asking Hillary to come over."

"That's different!" Addie snapped.

"Why?" Nick wanted to know. "Hillary's your friend. Tony and Jared are my friends."

"Miss T. knows Hillary," Addie answered.

"Miss T. could get to know Tony and Jared!"

"But they're not—they're not—"

"What?" Nick demanded. "They're not Christians? What are we, Addie, some little group that doesn't let in anybody who's not good enough for us? Do we make everybody pray before we let them hang around with us?"

When Addie didn't answer, Nick kept going. "I'm surprised you lowered your standards enough to let me in!"

"I'm almost sorry I did!" Addie snapped.

Nick whirled around in his seat and stared straight ahead. Brian, who had been silent through the entire argument, gave Addie a long, sad stare and turned around as well.

So much for holding my tongue, Addie thought bitterly.

CHAPTER 7

A Surprise Visitor

Brian had a dentist appointment after school, so Addie rode the bus home by herself that afternoon. When she got home, she went straight to her room and stayed there for half-an-hour. She lay face down on her bed, staring blankly out the window. *How could I have said such a thing?* she asked herself over and over. She tried to pray and couldn't. *Why would God want to listen to me?* she thought sadly.

There was a quiet knock at her door.

"Yeah?"

"Can I come in, sweetheart?"

No! she thought to herself. Out loud she said, "I don't care."

Her mother opened the door and stood at the foot of Addie's bed. "Brian's waiting for you outside, Addie."

"Tell him I don't feel good."

"Addie." Her mother's voice was stern. "I'm not going to lie for you."

"It's not a lie," Addie said glumly. "I wish I could die."

"Adlon Jane McCormick! Nothing is so bad that you have to talk like that."

"I told Brian he was too forgiving, and I told Nick I was sorry I lowered my standards and let him in my 'little Christian group.'"

Mrs. McCormick was too shocked to speak. She sank slowly to the bed and stared at her daughter in disbelief.

"So it's not a lie. I feel terrible."

"Addie, how could you?"

The disbelief in her mother's voice was too much for Addie and she choked back tears. "Mom, it's not my fault! You don't know what Nick's been like these past few days. All he wants to do is run around with the wrong kids. He never has time for Brian and me because he's got football practice or some meeting to go to. And yesterday he made fun of me—in front of all his friends—for being a Christian!"

Addie related the chain of events that had led to their argument that morning and her mother listened silently. When she was finished, Mrs. McCormick reached out to brush the thick black hair back from her daughter's face.

"It sounds like Nick is having a hard time adjusting, honey."

"Nick? What about Brian? His father is halfway around the world. He's here all by himself. And what about me? I'm not exactly crazy about going to another new school. I'm tired of hearing how hard it is for poor Nick! He's supposed to be a Christian now. Instead of getting mixed up with the wrong kids, he should be going to the Lord for help."

"Is that what you're doing?" her mother asked gently.

Addie didn't answer. She didn't want to tell her mother about the prayers that had bounced off the ceiling and back in her face just minutes ago.

But her mother knew. "It's not so easy, is it? And you've been a Christian for several years and you've lived in a Christian home all your life. So if it's hard for you sometimes, imagine what it must be like for Nick."

Addie only shrugged. Her mother continued. "Nick's parents love him very much, but I don't think they're Christians, so he can't really look to them for spiritual help. All he has are his Christian friends—you and Brian."

"I tried to tell him those other guys were bad for him today. That's when he threw it back in my face and said he was surprised I let him be in my 'little group.'"

Mrs. McCormick was silent for several long moments. "He has a point, Addie."

"Mom!"

"When you first met Nick this summer, we didn't stop you from riding bikes and visiting Miss T. together, did we?"

Addie shook her head. "But he didn't act like the guys at school act."

"Exactly. If he had, we would have talked with him, and with you, about what's appropriate behavior. We didn't have to do that because Nick knew what was right and what was wrong."

Addie sighed. "What's your point, Mom?"

Mrs. McCormick frowned. "Don't get smart, young lady. I'm trying to help you."

"I'm sorry."

"The point is, Nick needs to understand that the Lord has standards He expects us all to live by. Our friends, Christian or non-Christian, have to accept those standards and agree to them. Nick is right. God *wants* him to be friends with non-Christians. But he has to make sure those friendships follow God's rules, not someone else's. Not his football buddies'—and not yours either, Addie."

"Tony Knight and Jared Acker won't follow anyone's rules but their own, Mom."

"You may be right. But they deserve a chance, don't they? Maybe they've never been told there are different rules."

"And you think Nick's the one to tell them? You should have seen him yesterday! When they started making fun of me, he never said a word!" Addie still felt a knot in her stomach when she thought of the scene in the cafeteria.

"Addie, the Bible is full of people who turned their backs on God and everything they knew was right. God never gave up on them. He was always ready to take them back. Don't give up on Nick."

Addie nodded reluctantly. "I won't, Mom. It's just—hard to forgive." She sighed deeply.

Mrs. McCormick nodded and pulled her daughter to her feet. She held her close and prayed, "Lord, give Addie and Nick the grace they need to forgive one another. In Jesus' name, Amen."

"Amen," Addie echoed and smiled bleakly at her mother. "Thanks, Mom."

"Now go see what Brian wants." Her mother gave her a push toward the door and Addie went outside to meet her friend.

Brian sat under the sugar maple in the front yard, leaning against the trunk, his eyes closed. He sat up with a start when the screen door slammed.

"Hi." Addie spoke first, her fists shoved deep in the pockets of her jeans. "Are you very mad at me?"

Brian shook his head. "Of course not."

"I'll bet Nick's furious."

"Not really. I think he knows you didn't mean what you said." He paused. "Did you?"

"No!" Addie burst out. "I just lost my temper. He makes me so mad sometimes." She took a deep breath. "If you agree with Nick about letting Tony and Jared—and Hillary—see the secret room, I'll go along with you."

Brian smiled faintly. "Nick told me he didn't really want to bring them to Miss T.'s. I think he was testing you."

"And I failed the test royally."

"Just tell him you're sorry," Brian said. "He thinks he deserved what you said because of that mess in the cafeteria the other day. I told him you weren't trying to get even. You're just worried." He sighed. "So am I."

"Is he coming out to Miss T.'s after football practice?" Addie asked.

Brian shook his head. "I don't think he'll come back until you talk to him."

"I guess I don't blame him." Addie sighed. "When will he be home?"

"About four-thirty or quarter 'til five."

Addie glanced at her watch. "It's almost four-thirty now. It's probably too late to go to Miss T.'s anyway. We'll be eating supper in an hour."

"We have to go pick up our bikes."

Addie snapped her fingers. "That's right! I forgot we left them there. Did you walk here?"

Brian nodded. "We could walk to Miss T.'s if your mom will let you."

"I think she will if I'm with someone," Addie said. "I'll go ask."

Mrs. McCormick agreed to the walk on one condition. "Stay off the hard road. Walk in the ditch. I doubt if you'll meet any cars, but I don't want you to take any chances."

Addie and Brian set off down the ditch in the direction of Miss T.'s house. They had never traveled this path before and it was full of interesting diversions. Frogs were in abundance in the damp grass and they even saw the cocoon of a monarch butterfly attached to an old tree branch blown down in a storm.

Addie was so engrossed in examining the cocoon she barely noticed the only car to appear on the deserted road. It was long and black and seemed to slow down as it passed them. Brian watched the car curiously, but Addie only glanced at it.

"Addie." Brian poked her and pointed.

The black car had slowed almost to a stop. Then its back-up lights came on, and Brian and Addie exchanged a frightened glance.

"What should we do?" Addie whispered.

"I don't know," Brian whispered back.

The Cadillac limousine stopped even with Addie and Brian. The windows were tinted black, but Addie could make out a figure behind the wheel and one in the back seat. Then they heard the faint hum of a power window and Addie squealed with delight.

"Might I interest you in a ride, my dear girl?" asked Winston Rinehart with a smile.

CHAPTER 8

Bad News

"Hi, Mr. Rinehart." Addie was suddenly shy. She had only met the stately old gentleman once, and although his smile was warm, he was still *Winston Rinehart*!

Brian elbowed her in the ribs.

"Oh, Mr. Rinehart, this is Brian Dennison. He's a friend of mine and Nick's—and Miss T.'s," she added hastily. "He knows about... everything."

Winston Rinehart opened his door and eased himself out of the car slowly. He was a tall man, still thin, and his silver hair seemed to glimmer in the late afternoon sun. Addie and Brian climbed out of the ditch, and Brian and Mr. Rinehart shook hands.

"It's an honor to meet you, young man. Tee has already told me about you."

Brian colored slightly, but kept his composure. "It's an honor to meet you, too, sir," he said quietly.

"And Addie." Winston took one of Addie's hands in both of his and clasped it gently. He smiled and gestured toward the luxury automobile. "Please, ride with me to see Tee. She doesn't know I'm coming. I might get a better reception if I have her young friends with me."

Addie laughed. "Oh, she'll be glad to see you no matter what, Mr. Rinehart. We saw you on television the other day. She said then how much she missed you."

Winston nodded but his smile faded. "I'm eager to see her again as well. However, I'm afraid this visit is not going to be as pleasant as the last."

Addie's stomach did a little flip. "Why not?" she asked.

"Let's get to Tee's house and we can all talk then."

Addie nodded, and she and Brian climbed into the long, black limousine. There was a distinctive odor of leather and pipe smoke, and Addie's eyes grew wide as she looked around her. She'd never been in such a large, fancy car before.

The back of this limo had two seats facing one another, with a long, narrow oak table in between. Addie and Brian sat on the seat which looked out the back window. Winston Rinehart sat on the other, facing the children. The leather upholstery that lined the inside of the car was a deep, rich mahogany color, and there was a glass partition separating the passengers from the driver. Winston gestured to the chauffeur through this window, and Addie and Brian both squirmed around in their seat to get a good look at him.

"That's Wes—Wesley Riker," Winston said. Wes smiled and winked.

The car resumed its leisurely pace down the country road. Addie gave a deep, contented sigh and relaxed, enjoying the feeling of wealth and luxury.

The faint sound of classical piano music floated through the air and Brian's inquisitive eyes searched every inch of the car for speakers. There were none. Mr. Rinehart laughed at the young boy's curiosity.

"The speakers are hidden behind the upholstery," he said in answer to Brian's unasked question. "It mutes the sound quite a bit, but for old
folks like Tee and me, that's no problem."

"Why do you call her Tee?" Addie asked suddenly. "I mean, we call her Miss T. because it's
shorter, but I don't understand why you would
have to . . ." Her voice trailed off as she realized the
question might be too personal.

Evidently Winston Rinehart didn't find it so. "I
never knew Tee's real name was Eunice Tisdale," he
said. "I always knew her as Tierny Bryce. And as
I'm sure you would agree, Tierny was too stuffy a
name for such a down-to-earth person. So I short-
ened it to Tee."

He chuckled softly. "When our fans found out I
called her Tee, they picked up on it. But just plain
'Tee' was too simple for their idol, so they called her
'Miss Tee.' When I first heard you children address
her in the same manner, I was somewhat taken
aback. I imagine it gave her quite a start as well!"

Addie was amazed by this unexpected revelation. Miss T. had never told them about her nickname.

The new information didn't seem to affect Brian
at all. He was too busy examining all the other
features of the limousine and asking questions. "Is
the music on the radio or do you have a stereo
system in the car?"

Winston pushed a button on his side of the table
and the music stopped. A hidden panel slid open
and a compact disk lifted silently up and out of the
top of the table. He pushed the button again and the

disk returned to its hiding place, the panel slid shut, and the music resumed.

"Cool," was Brian's only comment and Mr. Rinehart chuckled.

The chauffeur made a smooth turn into Miss T.'s driveway and continued to the far end of the house. Brian opened the door on his side and jumped out, but Addie stayed where she was, hoping Mr. Riker would open the door for her. She wasn't disappointed. Winston remained seated while the chauffeur assisted Addie out of the car. She smiled and thanked him shyly. He winked again.

Brian beat her to the kitchen, but Miss T. was nowhere to be seen. Amy stood at the sink, up to her elbows in soapy water. She smiled when she saw the children.

"Hello, children. Miss T. is in the living room, watching the news. Go on in, I'm sure—"

She broke off abruptly at the sight of the two gentlemen at the back door. She looked questioningly at Addie and Brian, but they only grinned broadly. Drying her hands on a towel, she crossed the kitchen to the back door and opened it. When she saw who their visitors were, she took a deep breath and smiled graciously.

"Mr. Rinehart! What a pleasure to meet you! Eunice will be thrilled to know you're here. Come in, please."

"You must be Amy," Winston said as he stepped into the kitchen. "So nice to meet you as well. This is my driver, Wesley Riker. I'm sorry we popped in without warning, but I felt it was best, given the circumstances. Where is Tee?"

"In the living room—"

"Winston!" Miss T. entered the kitchen from the hall and gave her old friend a warm embrace. "What a surprise! Although I must admit, I've been thinking of you quite often these last few days." She motioned to the table. "Have a seat. Would you like some coffee?" Without waiting for an answer, she drew water at the sink and spooned coffee into the filter, talking all the time.

"I guess you've met Amy. She's my right hand. I don't know what I'd do without her. When we saw you on the news the other day, being grilled by the press, she's the one who kept her head when I panicked." She stopped for breath and looked at Winston's sober face. "Should I have panicked?" she asked dryly.

Winston tried to smile, but his eyes were sad. "I'm afraid things are getting a bit out of control, my dear." He sat down at the table, and Miss T. joined him.

Addie spoke softly. "We'll get our bikes and go on home, Miss T."

"No, no, dear, have a seat. You might as well hear what's going on." She looked around the room. "That goes for all of you. Sit down, please."

Addie and Brian sat across from the two elderly people while Mr. Riker pulled out a chair at the end of the table. Amy busied herself getting cups for everyone and putting water on to boil so the children could have hot chocolate. When the coffee was poured and the hot chocolate mixed, Winston began.

"I have tried my best to brush off questions about the discovery of your artifacts, Tee, but the media is relentless these days. When I refused to tell them where the props were found, they began to question my integrity!"

Winston's voice faltered, and for the first time, Addie saw a somewhat frightened elderly man, instead of a movie star. Quick tears came to her eyes and she felt a sudden rush of pity—and of guilt.

Miss T. saw the expression on the young girl's face and patted her hand gently. "None of that now, miss," she said. Winston continued.

"Can you imagine? Them, accusing me of wrongdoing? Of course, a number of people have tried from the beginning to find out how much the museum paid for the props and where the money went.

"When I offered to show them my books to prove I didn't get any money, they backed off. Jack Krueger came to my defense then, and told them the money had been placed in an account to help retired actors with living expenses."

Jack Krueger, Addie remembered, was the man who directed Rinehart and Bryce in most of their movies, and the friend who had helped Miss T. get out of Hollywood after her "death."

Miss T. smiled wryly. "Which is entirely the truth. I just hope he doesn't tell them which retired actor it's helping!"

"They have already tried to find out," Winston said. "When they were unable to get the name of the bank where the account was placed, they began to question Jack's word, as well."

Miss T. could only shake her head. The kitchen was quiet, except for the occasional gurgle of the old-fashioned coffee perculator. Winston pursed his lips and took Miss T.'s hand.

"I'm afraid it gets worse, Tee. Do you remember Conrad Carter?"

Miss T. frowned and shook her head. "No, I don't."

"He's the man who sculpted the statues for *Spies for Sale*. He saw the exhibit yesterday for the first time. He knows there is a statue missing, and he's accused me of keeping it for personal profit."

Miss T. was livid. "I remember him now," she fumed. "He was obnoxious 45 years ago and it sounds as if he's still obnoxious. Well, I don't want to cause more trouble. Take the statue, by all means. I only kept it for sentimental reasons."

Winston shook his head. "It's not that simple, Tee. If it shows up now, without an explanation, Conrad will be convinced he was right." Winston took a deep breath. "He's already threatened to sue me."

CHAPTER 9

Making Peace

This is all my fault, Addie thought bitterly. *Why can't I mind my own business? When will I ever learn!*

As if they could read her thoughts, Miss T. and Mr. Rinehart both turned to the young girl.

"Now, Addie," Miss T. began sternly. "I don't want you blaming yourself for this. No one is to blame but me. I'm the one who left 45 years ago. And if you hadn't discovered my secret, someone else would have. Do you understand me?"

Addie shrugged and nodded, but she couldn't look the elderly woman in the eye and she couldn't answer. She knew if she opened her mouth she might cry.

Winston reached across the table and took her hand. "And we will work this out somehow, my dear. Miss T. tells me you are quite a little girl of faith. We ask nothing of you but your prayers. Those will do us more good than any feelings of remorse or guilt on your part."

Addie looked gratefully at the old man and forced a small smile. "I won't *stop* praying, Mr. Rinehart," she said earnestly.

Miss T. nodded briskly. "I've seen what your prayers can do, miss. Speaking of answered prayers, where is Mr. Brady today?"

"Football practice," Brian answered.

"Again?"

Addie nodded. "You probably won't see much of him, except on Saturdays, remember? And you probably won't see us either, if we don't get home before dark. My dad won't be happy if I'm late two nights in a row."

"My goodness, it is getting dark. Get right home, both of you. In fact, call me when you get there, so I know you made it safe." Miss T. walked the children to the door and gave Addie a squeeze before they left.

The sun had dropped beneath the horizon and the crimson light that tinted the sky faded quickly. Addie didn't even slow down when Brian pulled into the Bradys' driveway. Two minutes later she skidded into her own drive and parked her bike quickly. There were headlights coming down the road, about a half-mile away, and she said a brief and heartfelt *Thank You, Lord!* just in case it was her father coming home from work.

Once inside, she made the phone call to Miss T. and hung up just as her father walked through the back door. He gave her a quick peck on the cheek. "Late again, huh, kiddo?"

"How'd you know?!"

"Saw your reflectors when you pulled in the drive. What's so exciting at Miss T.'s these days that you can't seem to make it home on time?"

Over supper, Addie told her father about the day's events, beginning with her fight with Nick on the bus that morning and ending with the visit from Winston Rinehart. She was afraid he might blame her for everything that was going wrong, but her father was unexpectedly sympathetic.

"Rough day."

Addie nodded bleakly.

"Winston's right, you know. Prayer will help them more than anything. And that includes Nick."

Mr. McCormick tilted his chair against the kitchen wall, folded his arms, closed his eyes, and began to pray. Addie laid her head on the table and Mrs. McCormick leaned against the counter. Mr. McCormick prayed at length for Nick and his friends, the troubles they had caused and the tension between Nick and Addie. Then he prayed for Miss T. and Winston and their unusual dilemma.

Addie listened quietly, agreeing in her spirit, and she felt more at peace than she had for several days. Whenever her father prayed like that, she could feel order coming back into her life and she thanked God silently for the parents she had.

* * *

Addie went to bed early that night and was almost asleep when she heard the phone ring. A minute later there was a quiet knock at the door. Her mother spoke softly into the darkened room.

"Addie? Are you asleep?"

"No. What's the matter?" Addie sat up and shook the cobwebs from her mind. "Who's on the phone?"

"It's Nick. He wants to talk to you. I know it's late, but I think this is important."

"Okay." Addie slipped her robe on and followed her mother down the stairs. She picked up the phone in the hall. "Hi. Nick?"

"Yeah. Hi." There was a long pause. "Look—"

"I'm sorry, Nick," Addie interrupted him. "I should be the one calling you. I was really awful to you this morning. I—I didn't mean a word of it and I—I hope you'll forgive me."

There was an embarrassed grunt at the other end. "I'm the one who's been pretty awful. I just don't know what to do. I mean, I want to be friends with the guys on the football team, but I don't want to be fighting with you and Brian all the time." He sighed.

"Me and my mom were talking about it this afternoon," Addie said. "She thinks you're right."

There was a stunned silence. "What?"

"I mean, she thinks it's okay for you to be friends with them. But you have to set the rules, not them," Addie explained.

"That's what Brian said," Nick agreed. "I don't know if I can do that. How do you think Jared and Tony will react the first time I tell them I have to do what the Lord wants me to do?"

Addie giggled. "We'll pick you up off the floor after they're through with you."

"That's what I'm afraid of," Nick said dryly. "Thanks a lot."

"What are friends for?"

She could hear Nick laugh softly to himself and she breathed a sigh of relief.

"Well, I guess I'll see you tomorrow."

"Okay. Thanks for calling, Nick," Addie said.

"Sure. Bye."

Addie hung up the phone and practically skipped into the kitchen. Her parents were sitting at the table, sipping steaming cups of coffee.

"Everything all right?" her father asked with a smile.

Addie nodded and pulled her robe close. "I only wish we could work out Miss T.'s problems as easy."

"Just keep praying, honey," her mother said.

Addie nodded. "I will. Well, see you in the morning."

"Good night, kiddo."

Back in bed, Addie snuggled under the covers that were still warm and smiled to herself. *Thank You, Lord*, she murmured. Her eyes closed and she was asleep before the *Amen* reached her lips.

* * *

The next morning on the bus, she and Nick exchanged embarrased grins, but nothing more was said about the previous day's events. Instead, Addie recounted her version of their limousine ride and the time spent with Winston Rinehart. Nick had heard it all the night before from Brian, but he was more than willing to listen to the story again.

"I feel sorry for Mr. Rinehart," he said when Addie had finished. "He got sucked into all of this just because he wanted to help Miss T. Now it sounds like the press is accusing him of being a crook. I know he isn't a real *big* star or anything, but he still has his reputation to consider."

Addie nodded. "And he can't do anything about it without exposing Miss T." She sighed deeply. "This one is going to take a real miracle." There was no argument from Brian or Nick.

Soon the bus lumbered into the school parking

lot. It stopped by the back door, where Jared Acker and Tony Knight were leaning against the brick wall, watching as kids poured out of the bus and into school.

"They're waiting for me," Nick said. He looked at Addie and Brian and took a deep breath. "Start praying," he said in a doomed voice.

"Hey, Brady," Tony said as the three friends left the bus. "Big plans for tonight. We're going to Acker's house after football practice."

"Why?" Nick asked in a neutral voice.

Jared grinned. "You're going to keep me company until my mom gets home. She works late tonight."

Nick seemed to consider the suggestion for a moment, then shook his head. "I don't think so. Not tonight."

"Why not?" Tony asked beligerently and fell into step beside Nick. That forced Brian and Addie to drop behind and Addie made a face but said nothing.

Nick looked back and nodded at Brian and Addie. "We've already made plans to go to a friend's house."

"Going to another prayer meeting, Brady?" Jared said wickedly.

"Yeah," Nick said with a friendly smile. "We're praying for you." This time his tone of voice made it obvious he wasn't joking and Addie had to smile to herself. She'd used the same line on Nick early in their friendship and it had had a similar effect then.

Tony and Jared tried to determine whether or not Nick was serious. When they concluded he was, they exchanged confused glances and quickened their steps. Nick dropped back to walk with Brian and Addie, and the three of them tried not to smile as they followed Tony and Jared into class.

CHAPTER 10

Trouble for Nick

Time seemed to speed by that week, probably because all the kids were busy. Nick had three more practices before the opening game Saturday. Addie and Brian spent their afternoons at Miss T.'s, sweeping the floor of the secret room and wiping down the walls. With Amy's help, they gave the entire room two coats of white paint.

Thursday afternoon on the bus, Brian plopped into the seat in front of Addie and handed her a piece of paper. There were a series of geometric shapes drawn around the edges of the page.

"Let's paint a border around the ceiling," he said.

Addie studied the paper carefully. "Won't these be hard to draw?" she asked.

"Not if Miss T. has a pencil, a yardstick, a ladder, and some cardboard."

Half-an-hour later, the children were rummaging through Miss T.'s kitchen drawers, looking for the necessary supplies. Amy helped them find everything they needed, including two ladders out in the greenhouse, and the children set to work immediately. Brian measured and drew patterns of squares, triangles, and rectangles out of leftover cardboard. He made one set for himself and another for Addie. They started in opposite corners and progressed around the room, painting the geometric shapes at random intervals.

Filling in the shapes was a time-consuming job so they decided to use only one color, purple, and soon the work was finished. The designs didn't look as crisp and sharp as they had on paper, but Addie and Brian were still pleased with the results. Even Miss T. was impressed.

"Good job," was her comment after scrutinizing their work. "It sure brightens up this room. Are you warm enough up here?"

Addie nodded. "It's fine, Miss T." She paused awkwardly. "Thanks again for letting us do this. I know it's been some trouble for you, to have the soffits fixed and the heat turned on, things like that."

Miss T. clucked under her breath and dismissed the girl's thanks with a wave of her hand. "I'd rather have you up here than a family of raccoons," she said with a smile and a wink.

* * *

Friday after school, Mrs. McCormick drove Addie to the Brady's house. "Nick's mom is going to take you to Miss T.'s," she said. "Dad will pick you all up around eight o'clock." The children were waiting for Nick today. Because the first football game was Saturday morning, he had a short practice. They were all going to eat supper with Miss T. so they could work late on their room.

Addie nodded. "Right. Bye, Mom."

Because they had to wait for Nick, Addie and Brian sat in the front yard and talked while they kept an eye on Jesse Kate for Mrs. Brady, who was on the phone. The toddler kept the two older children hopping.

One minute she was sitting quietly in a pile of leaves, contemplating a bug, and the next minute she was stuck under the picket fence. Then she found a pebble hidden in the grass and popped it in her mouth before Addie could stop her. When Addie tried to retrieve it, Jesse clamped her mouth shut tight. Brian made goofy faces so she would smile, and when she did, Addie slipped her index finger between the child's cheek and gum and pulled the pebble out quickly. Just as Jesse Kate began to squall, Mrs. Brady came out the door and took the unhappy little girl back inside.

"Thanks, kids," she called over her shoulder.

Addie tossed the rock toward the driveway and gave a sigh of relief. "How do mothers do that all day long?"

"Beats me. Makes you kind of glad to be an only child, doesn't it?"

Addie grinned and nodded. She glanced at her watch. "I wonder where Nick is? It's after four-thirty."

"Jared's mom was going to bring him home after she got off work. Maybe she was late."

"He went to Acker's after practice?" Addie couldn't keep the worried note out of her voice.

Brian smiled. "Relax. Jared's grandmother is visiting all this week. I heard them talking at noon. I guess she's pretty strict."

"Good." Addie was relieved. Jared Acker needed a strict grandma. Addie had two of them. She loved them immensely, but they watched her like a hawk whenever her parents had to be gone.

Just then a car appeared down the road and soon it turned into the Bradys' drive. Nick jumped out of the back seat and waved to Jared and his mother. The car backed out and sped away and Nick ran inside to change his clothes before he even greeted Addie and Brian.

"How's Grandma Acker?" Addie asked with a grin when Nick reappeared.

"Who?" Nick looked puzzled.

"I thought Jared's grandma was visiting this week," Addie said.

"Oh, yeah. She's okay, I guess." Nick brushed the question aside and opened the car door. "Come on, let's go. I'm anxious to see what you've done."

Once at Miss T.'s, Addie and Brian led Nick upstairs to the secret room. They opened the door and stepped back, watching Nick's reaction. They were disappointed.

"Well," he said hesitantly, "it's a lot cleaner. Nice and white. The walls look . . . good."

Addie sighed. "What is it, Nick? What don't you like?"

Nick shrugged. "I didn't know you were going to paint in a border. It's too purple. Why didn't you use any of the green?"

"It was easier—" Brian began.

"It doesn't look right," Nick interrupted rudely.

Addie frowned. "What's your problem tonight?"

When Nick didn't answer, Brian spoke up. "I've got an idea. Since Addie and I painted those shapes, maybe you could go around and paint another one in green."

Nick nodded. "Like a small circle. You've got too many straight lines."

Addie bit her lip to keep from snapping at Nick. Brian simply said, "Good idea," and used his pocket knife to make a rough pattern from a piece of cardboard left in the attic.

Nick used the pattern to put small green circles in and among the other shapes. He was working hard when Miss T. called them for supper. Before they went downstairs, Nick stood back to admire his handiwork.

"What do you think?" he asked Brian and Addie.

"Looks good," Brian said.

"Having some variety helps," Addie admitted reluctantly.

Supper was unusually quiet, although Brian made a valiant effort to keep a conversation going. Miss T. and Amy seemed to sense the redecorating project wasn't going well, and they steered the conversation to other topics.

"How's football practice, Nick?" Amy asked. "We've missed you."

"Practice is okay," Nick answered. He pushed his spaghetti around on his plate and nibbled his garlic bread.

"When is your first game?" asked Miss T.

"Tomorrow. Ten o'clock."

"Are we busy tomorrow, Amy?"

Amy smiled and shook her head.

Nick blushed. "Are you coming to the game?" he asked.

Miss T. nodded. "I'd like to see you play."

Addie was staring at the two older women in amazement. Miss T. saw her surprise and said, "Would you like a ride, miss? You *are* going?"

"No—I mean yes—I mean, I wasn't, but I will."

That surprised Nick even more. "I didn't think you'd want to bother."

Addie frowned. "I love football, Nick. You know that." Under her breath she added, "It's just some of the players I can't stand."

She didn't say it soft enough, because Brian shot her a warning look and Miss T. arched an eyebrow in Addie's direction.

Nick opened his mouth to protest, but Brian stopped him. "Is that your dad's car, Nick?"

Headlights were coming down the driveway, and soon Nick's father appeared at the back door. Amy rose to let him in.

"Come in, Mr. Brady," she said warmly. "I'm Amy."

"Hello," Mr. Brady answered. He nodded politely in Miss T.'s direction. "How do you do, Miss Tisdale? I'm sorry we haven't had a chance to meet before. Seems I'm always busy these days. Nick talks about you a lot."

Miss T. stood and the two shook hands. "That's perfectly all right, Mr. Brady. I feel I know you, too. Your son is quite a young man. We enjoy having him around."

The expression on Mr. Brady's face darkened. "I'm afraid you won't be seeing him for a while." He turned to Nick and spoke to his son for the first time. "Get in the car," he said roughly. "We have to go to the Ackers'. The police are waiting to talk to you and Jared."

Nick sat in shocked silence for only a second. Then his face turned bright red, he grabbed his coat from a chair and stalked out the back door.

Mr. Brady turned back to the stunned group at the table. "Good night," was all he said, and left. With a bewildered shrug, Brian slurped the rest of his milk and grabbed his coat from the chair. He followed father and son out the door and the two women and Addie watched them go in silence.

CHAPTER 11

The Game

"Well." Miss T. looked from Addie to Amy with worry in her eyes. "Is Nick having problems we don't know about?"

"I—I don't know." Addie's voice trembled and she took a deep, shaky breath. "I know he's been hanging out with some guys on the football team lately. At first he was so anxious to please them, I was afraid he'd do whatever they told him to do. But lately he seemed to have more of a mind of his own. I really thought he was going to be okay. I guess I was wrong."

"This might not be as serious as it sounds." Amy tried to speak with confidence, but Addie could hear the concern in her voice.

"I think it is," she replied. "Nick went home with Jared Acker after practice tonight. Jared's mom works late so they were by themselves." Addie paused, thinking. "Brian said Jared's grandma was there, visiting for the week. But when I asked Nick how Grandma Acker was, he acted as if he didn't know what I was talking about. Either she wasn't there, or they didn't go home."

"Well, from the look on his father's face, we might not be seeing Mr. Brady in a football game tomorrow," Miss T. said.

"I'll try to find out and give you a call," Addie promised. More headlights appeared on the road and she watched her father's car pull into the long drive and stop near the back door. The horn tooted softly and Addie glanced out the window.

"There are the coons again!" she exclaimed. She and the two women watched as three of the four animals scurried out of the headlight's glare and into the dark. The fourth coon, on his hind feet by the garbage can, gave the lid one last push with his nose and paws before he chickened out and followed the others into the woods.

Addie donned her coat and ran out the back door. "I'll let you know about tomorrow," she called over her shoulder. Miss T. waved and shut the door behind her.

"What's going on tomorrow, kiddo?" her father asked.

"Maybe nothing," Addie said glumly and told her father the news of Nick and his problems with the police.

Mr. McCormick said nothing, but he slowed down as they drove by Nick's home. The house was dark.

Addie's father shook his head sadly. "Poor kid," he said, almost to himself.

"Poor kid?!" Addie exploded. "Dad, we've been telling him and telling him this would happen. I thought he was beginning to listen, because things were going so well this week. Now this. He brought it on himself, if you ask me."

Mr. McCormick shrugged. "Maybe you're right," he said. "He does have to make the decision to stand up to those kids."

They pulled into their own drive and Addie pushed the button to open the garage door. The car glided smoothly into the garage and Mr. McCormick turned off the engine. Addie stayed where she was.

"I don't know if Nick can do that, Dad," she said sadly.

"He can, honey, but he needs to ask the Lord for help. And he needs to know you and Brian are going to be there for him when he does."

When Addie didn't answer, her father patted her hand gently and opened his door. "We'll pray about this tonight." Addie nodded.

For the rest of the evening, she called the Brady's every half-hour, with no luck.

Then the phone rang about 9:30, and Addie almost knocked over the hall lamp in her rush to answer it. It was Brian.

"Hi, Addie. Say, do you still want to go to the game tomorrow?"

"Nick gets to play? He's not grounded?" she asked incredulously.

"No, he's not. It's—it's kind of a long story," Brian answered. "I'll tell you about it tomorrow. But Nick has to leave early in the morning so I'm going to ride with Miss T. and Amy. Can you go?"

"Sure," Addie replied. "At least, I think I can. Hang on. Dad," she yelled at the top of her voice. "Can I ride with Miss T. and Amy to the football game tomorrow?"

Her father appeared in the door with a surprised look on his face, but he nodded. "Of course you can, honey."

"Yeah, I can go. Should I call Miss T.?" she asked Brian.

"No, I told her to plan on picking you up. If you weren't going, I'd just tell them in the morning. So, I'll see you then."

"What time?"

"Nine-thirty."

"Okay, bye." Addie hung up, turned to her father, and shrugged. "I still don't know what's happened, but Nick gets to play tomorrow, so his dad must not be too mad."

"That's a good sign," Mr. McCormick smiled. "But we'll still pray!"

"You bet we will," Addie agreed fervently.

* * *

The next morning Addie stood impatiently inside the kitchen door, eating her breakfast at the counter. She glanced out the window and down the road every few seconds. When Miss T.'s car appeared at the corner, she stuffed the remaining toast in her mouth and washed it down with the rest of her milk.

Since there were no other cars coming, she waited at the edge of the driveway and Miss T. simply stopped on the road. Addie was in the car and they were off in a matter of seconds.

"What happened?" she asked breathlessly.

"Good morning, Addie," Miss T. said wryly. "Why, I'm fine, thank you. How are you?"

Addie giggled. "Sorry," she said. "Hi, everybody." She turned back to Brian. "So, *what happened*?!"

Brian took a big breath and began his story. "Last night, the police got a call from a Mrs. Emma McCord.

She told them she had seen Jared Acker and another boy, someone she didn't recognize, coming out of her garage. She thought they were carrying some tools, so she went out to check, and sure enough, some of the tools her late husband collected were missing.

"Well, she suspected that other tools had been stolen a few days earlier, but she hadn't seen anyone until last night. When she saw Jared, she decided to call the police. They went to the Ackers and asked Jared who the other boy was. He told them it was Nick."

"I knew it," Addie said under her breath.

Brian looked at her in surprise. "Don't jump to conclusions, Addie. Nick said it wasn't him. After practice, he and Jared and Tony were going back to Jared's house. Tony and Jared told him they had a way to make some money and they were going to let him in on the deal. But they didn't tell him what it was.

"When they got close to Mrs. McCord's, Nick saw a mailbox and remembered he had a letter his mom wanted to mail from town. So he went to mail the letter. Jared told him where to meet them—Mrs. McCord's house. When Nick got there, he saw Jared and Tony running down the street and they were carrying a bunch of tools. He could hear Mrs. McCord yelling, but he couldn't tell what she was saying.

"Tony took off, and Jared and Nick went back to Jared's house. Jared told Nick they had been taking a few of Mrs. McCord's tools once or twice a week and selling them to Tony's uncle."

"How did Jared know they were there?" Addie asked.

"He mowed Mrs. McCord's yard this summer. That's why she recognized him. Anyway, Nick said he didn't want anything to do with the scheme and Jared got real mad at him. He told Nick if he ratted on them, Tony and him would get even.

"Well, of course, Nick wasn't going to rat. But when Jared told the officer it was him and not Tony, Nick got mad. So he told the police and his parents the real story. The police went to Knight's house to talk to Tony. Of course, he denied it, but they called Mrs. McCord and she identified him. They also found some of the tools in Tony's bedroom."

Addie sighed a tremendous sigh of relief. "So it wasn't Nick at all." She paused in the silence that followed. "I'm sorry. I guess I shouldn't expect the worst of Nick, but he's been so—difficult lately. I'm glad he finally stood up to them."

Brian nodded. "So am I. I just hope—"

"What?" Addie prodded.

"I hope they don't . . . get even."

Addie didn't answer. The prospect of what Tony and Jared might do was a scary one.

They arrived at the field and found seats just as Nick's team received the kick off. Addie pointed to one of the players.

"There's Jared," she said.

Brian nodded and pointed to another player on Nick's team. "And there's Tony."

Addie frowned. "I was hoping their folks would ground them. Like for the next ten years."

The offensive players of Nick's team took the field and Addie gave a small gasp of surprise. "Nick's the quarterback!" she exclaimed.

Brian nodded. "He's been dying to tell you Coach picked him to start the game. But he thought you didn't care."

Addie said nothing. On the first play, Nick handed the ball off to a running back and he ran up the middle for two yards. On second down and eight, Nick made a long pass to the split end, but an opposing player got a corner of the ball and it went out of bounds. Then it was third and long. Nick dropped back in the pocket to pass and suddenly a player appeared out of nowhere. He tackled Nick with a bone-crunching thud. Addie could hear Nick's startled grunt from where she sat. She watched in horror as he crumpled like a rag doll and lay motionless on the field.

CHAPTER 12

Troublesome Questions

There was a brief, eery silence and then several things happened at once. Both coaches went running onto the field. Mr. Stayton, Nick's coach, was shouting for a stretcher and motioning to Mrs. Parkin, the school nurse.

Out of the corner of her eye, Addie could see Mr. Brady flying down the bleachers and onto the field. But she couldn't take her eyes off of Nick. He still lay where he fell and he wasn't moving.

Miss T. reached over and took Addie's hand silently. Addie covered her eyes for a few seconds, then rubbed them hard and turned to Brian.

She had never seen Brian angry before and the sight startled her. His jaw was set so hard the muscles in his cheek were twitching. When he looked at her, his eyes were flashing and he found it hard to speak.

"I can't believe Tony would do something so low," he said between clenched teeth.

"Tony?" Addie glanced in confusion at the field.

"Tony was supposed to be blocking for Nick. He let that guy through on purpose. He *wanted* Nick to get hurt."

Addie hadn't been watching the offensive line, but she knew Brian was right. Tony was on the sideline with one of the assistant coaches, and he was getting the third degree. Then the coach gestured toward the sidelines and Tony stalked off, pulling his helmet from his head.

"Well, I guess he got even," Addie said softly. She felt sick to her stomach.

Just then Nick stirred and tried to sit up, but failed. Mrs. Parkin knelt beside him for several moments, checking all kinds of things that neither Addie nor Brian could see. Finally she nodded, and two men lifted Nick onto a stretcher and carried him off the field. The crowd applauded, Nick lifted his hand in a brief wave and was gone in an ambulance that had just arrived.

"Brian! Brian!" Addie could hear Mrs. Brady calling, but couldn't see her. Then she glimpsed Jesse Kate's blond curls and the two children ran down the bleacher steps to meet her.

"Brian, Addie, could you watch Jesse Kate for me?" Mrs. Brady pleaded. "I have to follow the ambulance to the hospital, and I just don't want to have to worry about Jesse."

"Of course," Brian and Addie both said. Brian took the little girl while Addie shouldered her diaper bag and grabbed the handful of toys Mrs. Brady thrust at her. The woman gave Jesse Kate a quick kiss on the cheek and was gone.

"Ma, ma, ma, ma, ma," Jesse Kate squealed in fright, but Addie distracted her by squeezing the horn on Mr. Nose, her favorite stuffed toy.

"Why don't we see if Miss T. will take us home?" Brian asked quickly. Jesse was already fighting to get down and smacking Brian on the face when she found she couldn't.

"No, no," Brian said firmly and took the little girl's hand. "Don't hit." Jesse frowned, but she stopped hitting and stuck her lower lip out at Addie.

"Good idea," Addie said.

They found Miss T. and Amy had already descended the bleachers and were ready to leave.

"There's no point in staying if Nick's not going to play," Miss T. said, so the four of them and Jesse Kate trooped back out to the car and headed for home.

On the way, Amy prayed for Nick and even Jesse Kate was quiet. They arrived at the Brady's in short order, and Miss T. made them promise to call with news as soon as they heard anything.

Addie fixed the three of them sandwiches while Brian played with Jesse. After lunch the little girl fell asleep at the table and Addie carried her cautiously to her crib.

Brian and Addie tried to keep their minds occupied by playing Monopoly and Trivial Pursuit, but Nick was never far from their thoughts. Finally, Addie flipped on the television and skimmed through the channels to see what was on.

"I love cable," she said. "You can choose from a whole lot of garbage instead of just a little."

Brian grinned. "Yeah, do you believe they spent a couple of thousand dollars for a dish, just so Mr. Brady could get the sports channel?"

"Look!" Addie exclaimed. "There's Winston!"

Winston Rinehart was standing in front of a large building, talking to reporters and smiling, as usual.

"I'm sorry Mr. Carter feels the need to make mountains out of molehills," he was saying. "I have never made any transactions concerning the statue in question. He is, of course, free to pursue whatever legal avenue he chooses, but I am afraid it will be for naught."

"Don't you love the way he talks?" Addie said.

Brian nodded. "I just hope he's right. I mean, you and I know Winston is innocent, but he might have to spend a lot of money to prove it."

"I've kind of forgotten about Miss T.'s troubles these last couple of days," Addie said with a sigh.

"I bet she hasn't," Brian said.

The phone rang and Brian leaped to answer it. Addie ran to the extension phone in the kitchen. It was Mrs. Brady.

"Nick's going to be fine," she said. "He was hit so hard he blacked out for a few minutes. He's also got a broken arm and some bruised ribs. The doctors are going to keep him overnight, just for observation."

Thank You, Lord, Addie said silently. Out loud she said, "Everything's okay here, too. Jesse is asleep."

"Oh, that's good. Listen, kids, Mr. Brady's coming home in a little while. I'm staying the night with Nick. He needs a few things, though. Brian, could you get some of his stuff together in a sack for me?" She gave him a list of items Nick had requested. "I've already talked with your father, Addie. He said he'd be glad to drive them in to the hospital for me. You two can come along with your dad and say hello to Nick if you'd like."

"Great!" Addie said and they hung up, much encouraged.

Addie phoned Miss T. with the good news and hung up just about the time Mr. Brady and then

Mr. McCormick pulled into the drive. Mr. Brady checked his daughter in her crib, then came out to the car to see the kids and Mr. McCormick off.

"Thanks a lot for your help," he said in a tired voice. "John, I really appreciate your doing this for me. I was up late last night and I'm so tired, I could curl up in that crib with Jesse and go right to sleep."

John McCormick smiled. "Maybe you should. And I'm glad to go. I'd be driving Addie in to see Nick regardless, right, kiddo?"

Addie just grinned. Her father knew her so well. Over lunch, she and Brian had rehearsed a very logical argument as to why they needed to visit Nick at the hospital.

The trip to town seemed to take forever, but soon they were in the hospital parking lot and then in the elevator that would take them to Nick's floor. There seemed to be a lot of commotion in the hallway outside the pediatric wing, but Addie paid little attention to it.

Brian dug in his pocket for the slip of paper that had Nick's room number on it. "Room 835," he said and began walking down the hall in that direction. They had almost reached Nick's room when a nurse came scurrying after them.

"Can I help you?" she asked breathlessly.

Mr. McCormick shook his head. "No. Room 835. We found it. Thanks, any—"

"Oh, I'm sorry," the nurse said with a secretive smile. "Nick has a very special visitor. You can't go in there right now."

At that moment, Mrs. Brady opened the door and saw them in the hall. "It's all right, nurse," she said. She was smiling broadly and she motioned Addie, Brian, and Mr. McCormick into the room. "We're expecting them. It's all right."

Addie slipped in through the open door and smiled with relief at the sight of Nick propped up in bed, sipping a glass of water. He looked very tired, but he was smiling. Then Addie saw why.

Winston Rinehart was by Nick's bedside and the older man smiled and winked at Addie and Brian. Mrs. Brady began to make introductions and Addie sucked in her breath. She had forgotten Nick's mom didn't know about the things that had happened in the last few months.

"I just can't get over how kind it was of Mr. Rinehart to stop and visit Nick here today. He's in town for the opening of that beautiful new theater arts building on the college campus tonight. But his agent had him booked to visit several wards of the hospital this afternoon. I'm just so thrilled that he picked Nick's room to visit!"

Nick began to look a little embarrassed at his mother's ramblings, but fortunately the nurse interrupted them just then. "Mrs. Brady? Your husband is on the phone. Would you like to take the call at the desk?"

Mrs. Brady frowned, obviously upset at being drawn away from such an exciting event. "Oh, well, I suppose I should," she said reluctantly. "But I'll be right back!" she said with a beaming smile at Winston.

He nodded graciously and Mrs. Brady left the room. Everyone breathed a sigh of relief and Winston shook his head. "I can see this is going to cause more problems than it's worth, so I'll simply say I'm very glad you're recovering, my boy, and I'll leave you to your friends."

"Thanks for coming, Winston," Nick said shyly.

"Think nothing of it, son," the old man smiled.

The door burst open and this time a tall, thin man in an expensive top coat entered without a word of explanation. He crossed the room quickly and pulled out a notebook as he forced his way between Addie and Brian and over to Nick.

He reached across the bed, grabbed Winston Rinehart's hand, and shook it briskly. The sleeve of his coat flapped in Nick's face and Nick made a disgusted sound and shoved it away.

"Mr. Rinehart, Kirby Roberts, the *Daily Gazette*. I've got a few questions I'd like to ask you, if you don't mind. I know you're scheduled to speak at the opening tonight and I wanted to catch you before you left."

"What is this?" Nick muttered from underneath the reporter's long arm. Kirby Roberts stepped back and looked at Nick, evidently surprised that there was a patient in the bed.

"Hello there, young man," he said gruffly. Then his eyes narrowed and he looked from Nick to the other people in the room. "What's your name? Who are you people? Are you friends of Mr. Rinehart?"

The blunt and unexpected questions took everyone by surprise and there was a long moment of silence.

CHAPTER 13

Change Is Coming

Before anyone could answer, the door burst open once again. This time a rather large, overbearing nurse with a stern frown on her face entered the room.

"Mr. Rogers," she began, "I believe you've been told several times—"

"Roberts," he corrected her.

"Whatever. You were told at the information desk not to harrass Mr. Rinehart while he's visiting patients. And yet I have had complaints from four different departments about your persistently rude behavior in attempting to question this gentleman. I'm afraid you will have to leave at once."

The reporter smiled a charming smile at the nurse and said, "I'm sure Mr. Rinehart will excuse the intrusion. I only have a few questions. What do you say, Winston?"

At the reporter's brazen use of his first name, Mr. Rinehart's thick, black eyebrows came together in a frown and he simply stared at the rude young man.

"*Now*, Mr. Rogers," said the nurse, pointing a finger at the door.

"Roberts," he muttered and paused at the end of Nick's bed to look at his chart. He scribbled something on his notebook and left.

"That was close," Addie said and Winston nodded his head in agreement.

"The sooner I leave, the better. This was not a good idea," he said. "Goodbye, my boy. I won't be seeing you again, at least for a time. Mr. Riker and I are leaving early tomorrow morning."

He shook hands with everyone and Mrs. Brady entered the room as he left. She couldn't hide her disappointment at his departure. When he kissed her hand instead of shaking it, she blushed and stammered, "Thank you—I mean—goodbye. Goodbye."

The door closed behind the stately old gentleman and Mrs. Brady sank into a chair in the corner, fanning her red face with her hand. "Oh, my," she said breathlessly. "What a charmer."

Nick just rolled his eyes and changed the subject. "I guess Tony got even, didn't he?"

"You knew he did that on purpose?" Addie asked.

"Yeah," Nick answered glumly. "Oh, well. It's over." He raised his right arm, now covered by a white cast. "And so is football, at least for me."

"Are you disappointed?" Brian asked him.

Nick shrugged. "Sure I am. But I'm kind of relieved, too. Now I won't get sucked into the kind of trouble I had last night. And I won't be arguing with you anymore," he said to Addie.

"I'm sorry, Nick," she said sincerely. "I never wanted something like this to happen."

"I know," Nick said. "Maybe this is the only way the Lord could get through to me, though."

Mr. McCormick shook his head. "You better be careful there, Nick. I don't believe the Lord causes these things to happen to kids."

"Of course He doesn't," Mrs. Brady put in indignantly.

"I do believe He can use them once they happen," Mr. McCormick continued. "You needed a reason to back off from some of the 'activities' your buddies were involved in. A broken arm probably wasn't your first choice, but since it's happened, you should try to use it to your advantage."

Nick nodded. "I will. Thanks for coming, you guys," he said. He tried to stifle a huge yawn and closed his eyes. "Here's your hat, what's your hurry," he murmured softly.

Addie and Brian both laughed at the expression, one of Miss T.'s favorites. They said goodbye and Nick waved without opening his eyes. Mrs. Brady walked them to the elevator.

"Thanks for everything," she said warmly. "You two are the best friends Nick's got. I'm glad you've stuck by him. Give Jesse Kate a kiss for me, Brian. Bye now."

The elevator chimed softly and Mr. McCormick and the children stepped in and pushed the button. When the door opened on the main floor, Addie stepped out and almost ran into Kirby Roberts.

"Just the people I wanted to see," he said jovially. "Mind if I ask you some questions?"

Mr. McCormick laughed. "Why us? You want to know what it's like to talk with Winston Rinehart? It was nice. Goodbye."

He sidestepped the persistent reporter and Addie and Brian followed him.

"I know you're acquainted with Mr. Rinehart," the reporter said behind them. "I overheard him in the bathroom this morning, talking with his driver before the press conference. He said he hoped to tell the children and Tee goodbye before he left tomorrow." He paused as Mr. McCormick, Addie, and Brian all came to a stop and turned to look at him. "Tee was the nickname he gave Tierny Bryce 45 years ago."

It took every ounce of self-control Addie had to keep from reacting to Kirby Roberts's words. She didn't even dare glance at Brian, and wisely, he kept from looking at her as well.

All Mr. McCormick said was, "Who?"

Kirby Roberts laughed shortly. "You heard me," he said knowingly, "and you know what I'm talking about."

Mr. McCormick shrugged. "I think you'd better go chase Winston Rinehart down. He might know what you're talking about."

He turned and walked out the hospital door. Addie and Brian followed him, but not before Addie saw a satisfied smile cross the reporter's face.

They walked quickly to the parking lot. No one spoke until they got in the car. Then Addie said, "Do you think he'll follow us, Dad?"

"No." Her father pounded the steering wheel in frustration. "No, he'll go back upstairs and try to question Nick. I'd almost bet on it."

"But Nick's asleep," Brian reminded him.

"And Mrs. Brady doesn't know a thing about this. If he asks her any questions, she'll be able to deny it all!" Addie grabbed onto that small thread of hope and clung to it. "Then he'll decide we're not the kids Winston was talking about and he'll go away."

She looked at her father hopefully and he ruffled her hair. "Maybe," was all he said.

The ride home was a quiet one. Once Mr. McCormick reached the city limits he bypassed the exit to the interstate. Instead, he took the state route. It was longer, but the view on the two-lane country road was much prettier. A river ran parallel to the highway and the trees that lined it still held a remnant of their brilliant fall colors.

Every few miles a lone farmhouse stood out against the grey sky. One was painted a crisp white and the outbuildings around it were clean and well-kept. Others were weathered and in need of repair. They met a few grain trucks bringing their last loads of corn to the local grain elevator, but most of the crops were in and the fields were empty.

It was a time of year that always made Addie sad, although she wasn't sure why. Winter wasn't far away and she loved the snow and the cold air and trips to the sledding hill. Her mother kept a fire in the fireplace on those days and coming home to a big cup of hot chocolate with melted marshmallows was one of her favorite things to do.

But it wasn't winter yet, only cold, damp fall. There were still the memories of summer and it was hard to say goodbye to the freedom of those days.

"What are you thinking about, honey?" Mr. McCormick broke into Addie's thoughts and the young girl sighed deeply.

"Why do things have to change?" she asked sadly. "I mean, this summer was perfect. The days were warm, but not too hot. It rained enough, but not too much. And then it was over."

"Fall's a pretty time, too," Brian said.

"I know," Addie agreed. "The trees were beautiful this year. Everything was red and gold and orange. I loved it. But now the leaves are almost gone. Why can't God just let us get to the prettiest time of the year and then stay there?"

Her father smiled ruefully. "He tried, honey. We're the ones who blew it."

"We sure did, didn't we?" she replied.

No one spoke the rest of the way home. The sun had hidden behind clouds all day and night fell quickly. It was dark when they dropped Brian off at the Bradys'.

"Give us a call if you need a ride to church tomorrow," Mr. McCormick told him.

Brian nodded. "Thanks. See you, Addie."

Addie waved and scooted over to the passenger side of the car. She buckled her seat belt and stared out the window.

"Things are going to start changing for Miss T." She spoke softly and her words were a statement, not a question.

"I'm afraid so, honey. I don't see how we can keep this whole thing a secret much longer. Maybe we never should have tried. But that wasn't our choice to make."

"Should we call her and tell her what happened today?" Addie asked her father.

He nodded. "I think it's only fair. If Kirby Roberts shows up on her doorstep, I'm sure she'll want to be prepared. I'll call her after supper."

"Thanks, Dad."

They turned into their own drive and the warm, yellow light in the kitchen window was a welcome sight. Mr. McCormick pulled into the garage and shut the car off. He reached over to give Addie a hug.

"Cheer up, honey. No matter what Kirby Roberts does, we have to remember, God is in control."

Addie hugged her father hard and prayed silently. *I'm glad it's You and not me, Lord.*

CHAPTER 14

"It's that
Rude Reporter!"

Bible class was buzzing when Addie and Brian slipped into their chairs the next morning.

"How's Nick?" was everyone's first question. Once his injuries had been described in detail, the next topic of discussion was the reason for his injuries.

"Tony really went overboard this time," Hillary Jackson said.

"He deserves to be suspended from school," added Mariel Cramer.

"They can't suspend him. The football league isn't associated with the school. But Mr. Stayton was really mad," said Andy Meeker, another boy in the class. "When he found out what was going on between Nick, Jared, and Tony, he called their parents. Tony and Jared might get kicked off the team."

"Did we win the game?" Addie asked.

"No," Andy sniffed. "They killed us."

After church, the McCormicks and Brian went out for lunch and then stopped at a video store and rented one of Nick's favorite movies. When they arrived at the Bradys', Nick was stretched out on the sofa in the living room. He sat up cautiously when they came through the back door.

He took the movie with a smile. "Thanks," he said. He glanced into the kitchen where Mrs. Brady was setting out coffee cups for the adults.

"I thought I was going to go crazy before you guys got here," he said in a low voice, all the while keeping an eye on the kitchen door. "You're not going to believe what's been going on!"

"Kirby Roberts," Brian and Addie said with one voice.

Nick was startled. "How did you know?"

"He was waiting for us when we left the hospital yesterday," Addie said. "My dad was afraid he'd go back to your room and bother you."

"Well, your dad was right. I was almost asleep when he came barging in again. Made my mom real mad. He kept trying to ask me questions. I'm lucky I had an excuse to act kind of ditzy. The medication *was* having an effect on me—I was real tired. But I made it look like I was off in ga-ga land.

"I might have overdone it. My mom kept looking at me real strange, and she finally called a nurse to get rid of the guy. She couldn't understand why I was acting the way I was or why this Roberts thought Mr. Rinehart knew me." He sighed. "I felt real bad not telling her the truth. I was hoping I could talk to Miss T. and ask her if we could let my parents in on the story."

Addie nodded. "I think we should tell them the whole thing. That Roberts guy knows a lot about Rinehart and Bryce. My dad thinks it's only a matter of time before he finds out everything."

"There's more," Nick said. "When we left the hospital this morning, I thought I saw Roberts following us in a white Toyota. I know it sounds crazy," he admitted, when Addie raised her eyebrows, "but I wanted to be sure. So I convinced Mom to pull over at a gas station to buy me a soda. The Toyota pulled into a parking lot across the street. I went in to buy the drink and guess who I ran into?"

"Who?"

"Winston Rinehart's driver! They were filling up the limo before they returned it to the car rental at the airport. I told him I thought Roberts was following me, so we didn't talk long and he went out the back way. The limo was parked behind the station. When Mom and I left, I watched to see if the Toyota followed us, but it went in the opposite direction."

"That's good." Addie was relieved.

"No, that's bad," Nick said. "He followed the limo."

"Mr. Rinehart knows how to take care of Roberts," Brian said confidently. "I'm just glad he didn't follow you home. At least he doesn't know where you live."

"It won't be long before he finds out," Nick said glumly. "I've seen a white Toyota drive by twice this morning. Dad was gone, so our car wasn't out. But it is now. If he drives by again, he'll see it."

"He's not looking for you, Nick," Addie said slowly. "When he stopped us yesterday, he told us he overheard Mr. Rinehart talking about 'Tee and the children.' He's assuming we're the children. Now he's looking for Miss T."

"But we're his link to Miss T.," Nick reminded her.

"I think Nick's right, Addie," Brian said and nodded toward the large picture window at the front of the room.

As if on cue, a shiny white Toyota pulled into the driveway and Kirby Roberts stepped out of the car.

He checked the license plate on the Bradys' red Subaru and then hurried to the back door.

Even though the children watched every step he took, they all jumped at the sound of his sharp knock. From the kitchen, they heard Mrs. Brady's disgusted gasp.

"It's that rude reporter I was telling you about yesterday," she said to Mr. Brady. "He just won't leave us alone. And all because that movie star stopped in Nick's room yesterday!"

"I'll get rid of him for good," Mr. Brady said sharply. "It's going too far when reporters harrass kids just to get some scoop on a has-been movie star!"

"Bill, wait." Mr. McCormick's tone was urgent and Bill Brady looked at him in surprise.

Addie's father took a deep breath. "There's more to this than you're aware of. Answer the door, but if Roberts asks any questions, let me answer. We'll explain everything after he's gone, but while he's here, I'll do the talking. *Please*. Trust me."

Mr. and Mrs. Brady exchanged a long, confused glance, but finally Mr. Brady gave a short nod and opened the door.

"Mr. Brady, my name's Kirby Roberts, from the *Daily Gazette*. I met your son and your wife yesterday, and I wondered if I might follow up that meeting with some questions I have. It's for an article in next Sunday's paper."

When Mr. Brady didn't answer, Kirby Roberts put a tentative foot in the door. "May I come in?"

Nick's father shrugged and stood aside. Kirby Roberts stepped into the room and smiled at the adults sitting at the table. He glanced past them to the children in the living room and winked.

"I'm looking for Miss Tisdale," he said without any pretense.

Nick's mother opened and shut her mouth silently, then looked at Mr. McCormick.

"Tisdale?" John said with a puzzled frown. "What's the first name?"

Kirby Roberts's smile faded and he dug in several pockets before he found a crumpled piece of paper. "Martha," he answered. "Martha Tisdale."

Mr. McCormick nodded. "Right. Martha Tisdale. Well, I'm sorry to tell you, Miss Tisdale died about five years ago."

"What?" The brash reporter frowned and crammed the paper back in his front coat pocket. "She *died*?"

"Yep. Five years ago."

Kirby Roberts sighed. "You're sure of that?"

"Well," Mr. McCormick drawled, his expression deadpan, "they buried her. I hope they were sure."

Addie stifled a giggle and Mrs. McCormick poked her husband. "John," she said reprovingly.

Roberts stared out the window for several seconds. "Where did she live?"

Mr. McCormick pointed in the general direction of Miss T.'s house. "That way."

Roberts frowned at the deliberately vague answer and his eyes narrowed. "Who lives there now?" he asked, watching Mr. McCormick closely.

Addie's father frowned again and looked at his wife. "You've met her, haven't you, honey?"

Mrs. McCormick hesitated, then said, "The Japanese woman?"

"Right."

"Oh, what is her name? Yamaguchi? Takasushi? Something like that." Mrs. McCormick shrugged and gave the reporter a bright smile.

Roberts shook his head slightly and looked in turn at Mr. and Mrs. Brady. The genuine confusion on both their faces was proof enough they had no idea what was going on.

"Okay." Roberts gave John McCormick another long, piercing look. But Addie's father had a poker face and the reporter seemed to silently acknowledge defeat. "Thanks for your time."

He shook hands with Mr. Brady and left. They all watched in silence as the little white car pulled out of the drive and headed back toward town.

Mrs. Brady was the first to break the silence. "What is going on?" she demanded and gave Addie's father an accusing look. "Miss Tisdale is not dead!"

"Eunice Tisdale is not dead," he corrected her. "Martha Tisdale is, in fact, dead and buried."

"Who's Martha Tisdale?" Mr. Brady asked.

"Eunice's sister."

"Why didn't you want to tell him Martha Tisdale had a sister? And why did you imply only Amy lives in the house now?" Mrs. Brady was frowning and shaking her head.

"Kids," Mr. McCormick called softly. "I know you're listening. Why don't you come in here and help me out?"

Addie, Nick, and Brian filed silently into the kitchen and took seats around the table.

Mr. Brady studied their sober faces. "Someone had better start doing some explaining."

John McCormick closed his eyes and rubbed the spot on his forehead he always rubbed when he had a headache. He look up at the Bradys with a rueful smile. "Got any more coffee?"

CHAPTER 15

Roberts Returns

The silence at the Bradys' kitchen table was broken only by the sound of the soft, persistent *honk-honk* of Mr. Nose from the nursery.

"Jesse Kate's awake," Addie said.

Nick's parents both stared at her blankly. Then Mrs. Brady shook her head slightly and stood up. "I guess I should go get her."

She left the table, but paused in the doorway and looked back at Mr. McCormick. "A movie star?" she asked increduously. "Tierny Bryce?"

Mr. McCormick smiled and nodded and Mrs. Brady left the room, still shaking her head.

Mr. Brady stared at his son, but Nick couldn't meet his father's eyes. "You've known about this for months," he said quietly to the boy.

Nick nodded.

Mr. Brady reached over and grasped Nick's shoulder. "Don't worry, son. I'm not mad at you. I'm— I'm proud of you," he said gruffly.

Nick looked at his father in surprise.

"That's quite a secret to keep," the older man continued. "But you did it because you were more concerned about Miss T.'s welfare than your own interests. That takes some maturity."

Nick took a deep breath and a small smile played around the corners of his mouth. He studied the wood grain of the table intently, then traced it with his finger. "Thanks," he said softly.

Mrs. Brady came back to the kitchen with Jesse Kate. The toddler's tousled blond head was pillowed on her mother's shoulder. Addie smiled and waved at the little girl and blew her a kiss. Jesse blew a kiss back and then buried her head in embarrassment. Everyone laughed.

"Well, we'd better head for home," Mr. McCormick said. "I need to call Eunice and tell her about Kirby Roberts and about our discussion today."

"Will you be at school tomorrow?" Addie asked Nick as they left.

"Sure," Nick said. "I'm just a little sore. It's not bad enough to keep me out of school." He sighed. "But I'm not looking forward to it," he said.

Brian spoke up. "We'll be there for you," he said bluntly. Addie nodded in agreement.

"Good," was all Nick said.

* * *

The next day was a rough one for Nick. His ribs hurt more than he wanted to admit, and sitting for long periods was painful for him. Even more painful, though, were the dark looks and cutting remarks Jared and Tony directed his way every chance they got. Word had gotten out that both boys were suspended from the next game.

Nick did his best to ignore it all. When lunch came, there was an obvious division in the cafeteria. Tony, Jared, and a few of the other football players took over a table at the far end of the room.

Almost everyone else stopped to say hi to Nick and he spent most of the hour having his cast signed.

But his expression was troubled and he pulled Addie to one side when lunch was finished. Some kids had wandered out to spend the last 15 minutes in the gym, but most still sat around the tables. Jared and Tony sat alone at the other end of the room, picking at the food on their trays. The other football players had left.

"How do you let someone know you forgive them?" Nick asked Addie.

Addie glanced at the two lone boys and frowned. "You sure you want to?" she muttered and then was sorry she'd said it.

"Come on, Addie. You know I've got to, even if I don't feel like it."

"Yeah, I know," she answered. "I'm not sure, Nick. I mean, you can't act like it never happened. You have to find some way to let them know you didn't like what they did, but you're willing to forget about it."

Nick nodded. He took a deep breath and squared his shoulders. "Okay," he said. "You and Brian wait for me, okay?"

"Sure," Brian answered and Addie nodded.

"Pray for me, too," Nick added in a much lower voice and walked across the room to where Tony and Jared sat.

Neither boy looked up as Nick approached their table, but he sat down anyway. Addie couldn't hear a word that was being said and that frustrated her so she settled for some silent words of her own. *Help him say the right thing, Lord.*

The noise in the cafeteria lessened considerably as many of the other kids watched Nick confront the two boys. It appeared that Nick was doing all the talking. Finally he stopped. There was no response from Tony or Jared, so Nick stood up and said something else. Tony finally acknowledged Nick by looking at him and nodding. When Nick left, Tony gave a slight wave of his hand and Nick said, loud enough for everyone to hear, "See you around, guys."

"Yeah," they both answered.

Nick walked back to his friends and the expression on his face was one of satisfaction.

"What did you say?" Addie whispered when Nick was close enough to hear.

He just grinned. "Enough," he said, and that was all they could get out of him.

* * *

That day after school, Addie changed her clothes quickly and rode down to Nick's house. The air was brisk, even cold, and she realized with a start that their days of riding bikes to Miss T.'s were limited.

What are we going to do? she wondered, annoyed with herself that she'd never thought of the problem before. *We'll have to find a way there! We're just getting our secret room the way we want it and Nick's not in football anymore and—Nick!*

The sudden thought of Nick and his cast shocked her even more. Nick couldn't ride to Miss T.'s in a cast.

She pulled into the Bradys' drive and dropped her bike in the grass with a dejected sigh. Mrs.

Brady opened the back door with Jesse Kate in her arms.

"Come on, Addie," she said with a bright smile. "The boys are waiting. I'm going to drive you to Miss T.'s. I spoke with her earlier. We had quite a nice talk, actually. She's got some old furniture she wants to give you for your secret room, if you're interested. And she wants you to get it upstairs today, so I told her I'd bring you all over. I think your father will pick you up after he gets home."

"Thanks," Addie said gratefully.

When they arrived, Miss T. and Amy made the proper fuss over Nick and his cast. They both signed it and Miss T. insisted on giving Nick some cookies and milk and settling him on the couch while they discussed what furniture the children wanted to take upstairs.

There was an old black table with legs on wheels, a brown recliner that had the upholstery worn off on the arms and the footrest, a rocking chair in fairly good condition, a desk chair on wheels, two matching end tables, two matching brown lamps, and several rag rugs.

The children studied the furniture in silence.

"I know it's old—" Miss T. began in an apologetic voice.

"It's great!" Brian interrupted her.

Addie agreed. "Can we use it all?" she asked.

Miss T. laughed in relief. "Well, of course you can," she exclaimed. Then she frowned. "But I certainly can't help carry it upstairs and I'm not about to allow Nick to do any lifting. That just leaves the three of you."

"We can do it," Amy said confidently as she made a muscle with her right arm.

With Amy's help, they managed to get all of the furniture, except for the recliner, to the attic in short order. It was more awkward than it was heavy, and they soon had the freshly painted room arranged to their liking.

Brian wanted the table and desk chair directly under the west window. "We can put my computer here and we won't need any extra light," he explained.

The rocker, an end table, and a lamp went in one corner, and the second end table and lamp went in the other corner. "That's so two of us can read while the other works on the computer. But we'll have to wait to bring the recliner up," Addie said. "My dad will help us. Maybe even tonight if he gets here pretty soon."

As if on cue, there was the faraway sound of someone banging on the door two floors below them.

"He's early," Miss T. commented, glancing out the window at the slowly fading sunlight.

Addie shook her head slowly. "My dad shouldn't be off work quite yet. And he wouldn't keep banging on the door like that."

Whoever was at the door was persistent. They knocked hard several times, waited a second or two, then knocked again. This pattern continued but no one moved to go downstairs.

"It's Kirby Roberts," Brian finally said.

Miss T. nodded. "I think you're right." She glanced at Amy. "I thought I was ready to meet this man, but now I'm not sure. Amy, could you—?"

Without a second's hesitation, Amy nodded and was out the door and down the attic stairs.

All three children looked at Miss T., but she shook her head at the unasked question in their eyes. "No. Please stay here with me."

They all sighed. Only Brian moved closer to the door and he stayed there, straining to hear what was going on downstairs.

The unmistakable sound of Kirby Roberts' voice floated up the stairs, but his words were indistinguishable. Then Amy's soft voice replied. She talked for what seemed like ages, then Roberts said something else.

Their exchange went on forever, and even Miss T. grew tense as time went by. Finally, they heard Amy's soft footsteps on the attic stairs.

A chorus of voices greeted her before she stepped into the room and she held up her hand for silence. They quieted immediately.

"He's gone," she said.

"What did he want?" Miss T.'s voice trembled at the question.

"Who," Amy corrected her. "Eunice Tisdale."

"He knows my name now," Miss T. said sadly. Amy nodded. "What did you tell him?"

Amy paused slightly before answering. "Everything," she said simply.

Shocked silence greeted her unexpected revelation. Then Miss T.'s hand went to her heart and her color faded.

Addie moved quickly to put an arm around the old woman. "Amy..." the young girl whispered.

"Everything?" Miss T. repeated. "I mean ... *everything*?"

Amy nodded.

Suddenly Addie felt the old woman sit up and some color came back to her face. "But he left," she said sharply. "Why did he leave?"

Amy shrugged and gave her elderly friend a mischievous smile. "I guess he doesn't understand Japanese," she said.

CHAPTER 16

Miss T. Tells All

Miss T. began to laugh, and she laughed so hard tears rolled down her cheeks. Relief flooded through the children and they began to laugh as well. Only Amy kept her composure, but she smiled at them, looking very pleased with herself.

When Brian finally caught his breath, he gasped, "You told him everything—in *Japanese*?"

Amy nodded. "I knew I could not bring myself to tell him an outright lie. So I prayed and asked the Lord to show me how I could be honest and still protect Eunice. When I answered the door and Mr. Roberts asked me if I knew of a Eunice Tisdale, I opened my mouth—and out came Japanese."

Nick was holding his bruised ribs. "Oh, man, do my sides hurt! Amy, you're brilliant. I'm surprised he didn't ask you if you spoke English."

"Oh, he did," Amy answered. "And I told him I spoke perfect English."

"In Japanese," Addie finished for her and started giggling again.

"Sounds like you're all having fun," said a deep voice from the doorway and everyone jumped.

"Oh, Dad," Addie squealed, "you scared us."

"Sorry," he grinned, "but I knocked at the door and no one answered, so I let myself in. I was a little worried about you. I saw Kirby Roberts's car pull away from the house, Eunice. Then I heard all the merriment up here and I couldn't resist sneaking up on you."

"Kirby Roberts just now left?" Addie asked, surprised. "What was he doing hanging around here?"

"Maybe he hoped to see something . . . or someone." Mr. McCormick looked at Miss T. "But he's gone now."

He stepped into the room and the children crowded around him, eager to tell him about Amy's ingenuous solution to Kirby Roberts's probing questions.

"The Lord always provides a way, doesn't He?" Mr. McCormick chuckled.

"And I appreciate both of you finding those ways," Miss T. said, "but I can't ask you to continue compromising the truth to protect me. I have to stop this charade. Tonight I'm going to work on a statement explaining everything and I'll take it to the newspaper myself. I'm not going to give some nosy reporter a scoop if I can help it."

Miss T.'s proclamation sobered everyone up in a hurry. Mr. McCormick reached out and took the old woman's hand.

"I think that's the best thing you can do," he agreed. "If Roberts knows about Eunice Tisdale now, it won't be long before he puts all the facts together himself."

Miss T. grasped his hand tightly and couldn't speak for several seconds.

"What can I do to help?" Addie's father asked gently.

"Go with me when I do this," Miss T. answered.

"Of course. Whenever you're ready."

"Tomorrow. At noon."

Mr. McCormick nodded, but Addie couldn't keep a small exclamation of disappointment from escaping her lips.

Miss T. smiled at the crestfallen expression on the children's faces. "You want to go along. I should have thought of that myself. What time are you out of school?"

"A little after three," Addie said.

Miss T. turned to Addie's father. "Can we wait until three and pick them up before we go to the newspaper?"

Mr. McCormick nodded again. "That can be arranged," he said with a smile.

"Well." Miss T. stood up and smoothed out the skirt of her dress. "I'm glad that's settled. I'm hungry. What's for supper, Amy?"

With her mind made up, Miss T. seemed to have a weight lifted from her shoulders. She made small talk with Mr. McCormick on the way downstairs and bid the children a cheerful goodbye at the back door.

The ride home was a quiet one. Mr. McCormick spoke first.

"Your secret room looks real nice," he commented. Silence.

"Thanks," Brian finally said. "Say, do you think you could help us—"

"I don't know about you guys," Nick interrupted his friend, "but I'm scared. I mean, what's going to happen to Miss T. now?"

No one had an answer. Mr. McCormick cleared his throat. "Well, Nick, obviously we can't predict the outcome of all this. But we don't need to be scared. The Lord will take care of Miss T. All we need to do is—"

"Pray," Nick finished for him. "I know."

* * *

Prayer was the only thing that got the three children through school the next day. Addie missed several questions on her math test when she skipped a line on the answer sheet and put the answers to questions seven, eight, and nine on lines eight, nine, and ten.

Nick was more absentminded than usual and Mrs. Himmel finally sent him to the nurse, convinced his injuries from the previous Saturday were still bothering him.

Even Brian's thoughts wandered, and he missed the transition from History to English. When Mrs. Himmel asked him to open his text and begin reading on page 82, he read an entire paragraph on Gettysburg before the teacher stopped him.

"Brian," she said dryly, "the Civil War is over, at least for today. Why don't you join the rest of us in the twentieth century and read the poem by Shel Silverstein on page 82 of your *English* book?"

"Whew!" Brian exclaimed as they met outside the school building after the final bell. "I thought this day would never end."

Addie's father, Miss T., and Amy were waiting in the car next to the schoolbus that normally took the children home. The children climbed into the back seat and Miss T. handed Addie two sheets of yellow legal paper covered front and back with neat, black printing.

"Read this," she commanded by way of greeting. "Tell me if you think it's accurate."

Addie read through both sides of the first page quickly and handed it to Brian. He and Nick read that while Addie finished the second page.

The first half was a fairly detailed account of the events which led to Tierny Bryce's alleged death. One brief sentence covered the 45 years between that time and the present. *I lived peacefully for many years in our family home with my late sister, Martha.*

The second half chronicled the events of the last three months, finishing with an explanation of the reason for the missing statue from the exhibit in New York and her desire to clear the names of her good friends Winston Rinehart and Jack Krueger.

When the children finished, Addie handed the pages back over the front seat. "That's—very good," she said awkwardly.

"Nothing missing?" Miss T. demanded.

"Not that I can think of," Addie said, and Brian and Nick nodded.

"Good." Miss T. settled back, satisfied, and they rode the rest of the way to town in silence.

The office of the *Daily Gazette* was a formidable three-story granite building with a glass front. The setting sun was reflected in the dark glass and the children spoke to one another in soft whispers before they even got inside.

Once there, they were even more impressed. It was one huge room, probably as big as three school gymnasiums, and completely open. The marble floor was dotted with large, shiny wooden desks and there were well-dressed men and women moving confidently around the room, over to the glass elevator, in and out of the building.

There was no ceiling. The room was open to the top of the building, and as Addie gazed up three stories, she could hear the plastic clacking of word processors on the balconies above. The low din of voices muted by distance filled the room.

They all hesitated inside the front door, stopped momentarily by the magnitude of it all. Then Miss T. shook her head as if clearing away cobwebs and marched purposefully to the first desk. Mr. McCormick matched her stride and the children followed.

The attractive woman behind the desk gave them a pleasant smile. "May I help you?"

"I need to see the editor," Miss T. announced. "As soon as possible, please."

The pleasant smile faded just a bit and the woman asked politely, "Do you have an appointment?"

"No."

The woman was startled by the curt answer and she looked briefly at Mr. McCormick.

"This really is very important. We have some information I'm sure he'd be interested in," Mr. McCormick said.

"And what is the nature of that information?"

"It is a . . . press release on a very . . . timely subject," Mr. McCormick answered. "We'd rather not say anything more until we can speak with the editor."

"I'm sorry, but Mr. Peterson requires an appointment for his visitors. He's a very busy person—"

"We all are," Miss T. interrupted sharply.

A distinguished gentleman in an expensive suit was leaving the building. He overheard the exchange between the two women and approached the desk.

"I was on my way out for some coffee, Jane," he said. "Is there anything I can help you with before I go?"

"Thank you, Mr. Sutton, there is." She turned back to Miss T. "This is Mr. Sutton, our Features Editor. Perhaps he can help you."

Addie's father and Miss T. exchanged a quick glance. Mr. McCormick nodded slightly.

"Very well," Miss T. snapped. "Where's your office?"

The man opened his mouth slightly, then closed it and smiled a tight smile. "This way," he said and led them across the marbled floor to a large oak door.

His office was a spacious room, with several big leather chairs and a globe on a stand that lit up when he turned the lights on. The walls were covered with newspaper articles in brass frames and two crystal chandeliers hung from the ceiling.

Miss T. followed Mr. Sutton across the room to his desk.

"I'd like you to read this," she said and handed him the yellow paper.

He took it without a word and settled into his chair. He waved to the variety of seats around the room. "Please," he said.

Mr. McCormick and the children sat down on four chairs grouped together behind a long, oak coffee table. Miss T. remained standing in front of the imposing desk.

The editor read her story without stopping and his expression never changed. When he finished, he lay the papers quietly on his desk and leaned back in his chair. He gazed curiously at Miss T. for several moments and under his unflinching stare Miss T.'s bravado faltered.

"You—you don't believe me," she finally said. She groped for the chair behind her and sank into it slowly. "I have gone over this moment a thousand times in my mind. Never once did I realize how crazy it would sound!" She began to laugh, genuinely laugh, and Mr. McCormick moved quickly to her side.

"Eunice," he said gently.

"I know, I know," she said and wiped her eyes. "He'll think I'm a real loony if I don't get control of myself."

Addie began to giggle, than Nick, and Mr. McCormick shot them a warning glance.

"I haven't said I don't believe you," Mr. Sutton said. "In fact, I'm taking this very seriously in light of the news article we published in this morning's paper."

Miss T.'s laughter stopped abruptly. "What article?"

Mr. Sutton picked up a newpaper on the edge of his desk, opened it to an inside page, and handed it to the elderly woman. Miss T. read the headline of the article he pointed to and gasped softly.

Mr. McCormick leaned over the old woman's

shoulder to read and his eyes widened.

"Dad!" Addie whispered urgently and her father turned to the children. His expression was grim.

"Winston Rinehart is missing," he said.

CHAPTER 17

But Can She Prove It?

The initial shock lasted only a second, then all three children crowded around Miss T. Addie read aloud bits and pieces of the article the old woman held in her trembling hands.

"... When Winston Rinehart and his personal secretary and chauffeur, Wesley Riker, did not arrive home Sunday evening as planned, Helen Riker contacted authorities to report the absence of her husband and the retired actor.... Airline officials in Illinois reported that neither man boarded Flight 121 to Chicago.... Their whereabouts at this time are unknown.... After 24 hours, authorities in New York and Illinois have declared both men legally missing and an investigation is underway."

"Who in the world would want to kidnap Winston?" Nick exploded.

"How do you know he's been kidnapped?"

"Why else would he disappear?"

"Maybe they had an accident."

"Someone would have seen it!"

"Children, children!" Miss T. clapped her hands sharply and the noisy debate ceased. "Let a body think! What could have happened?" Her voice trailed off and she stared vacantly out the plate glass window. Finally she shook her head. "This is so preposterous! Everyone liked Winston. I mean, I know he's had his problems with Conrad Carter lately, but—"

"That's right!" Nick exclaimed. "That guy thinks Winston has his statue."

Miss T. frowned at the interruption and Addie clapped her hand over Nick's mouth.

"But Conrad was always a sly man. He's too smart to do something so obvious," Miss T. continued.

"Unless that statue has more significance than we're aware of," Mr. McCormick said.

Mr. Sutton had been listening intently to the heated conversation and now he stood up and walked around the desk to where Miss T. sat. There was a smile on his face and a glow in his eyes, and everyone realized any doubts the editor might have had about Miss T.'s story had been dispelled.

He clasped Miss T.'s hand gently with both of his. "Tierny Bryce," he said softly. "Welcome back!"

Miss T. nodded curtly. "Thank you, Mr. Sutton," she said.

"I'm honored that you chose to bring your story to our paper, but I must say I'm puzzled. Why didn't you go to one of the local TV stations?"

"I was afraid that nosy reporter of yours would beat me to it!" she exclaimed.

Mr. Sutton frowned. "And who might that be?"

"Kirby Roberts."

"Roberts...Roberts," Mr. Sutton repeated. "Just a minute." He crossed quickly to his desk, picked up the phone, and punched a button. "Jane, would you get in the computer and pull up the file on one of our reporters for me? His name is Kirby Roberts."

There was a pause, then Mr. Sutton nodded. "Roberts, right." Another long pause. "Thank you, Jane, that's what I thought." He hung the phone up and turned back to Miss T.

"I'm afraid someone's been deceiving you. We have no reporter named Kirby Roberts."

There was another stunned silence.

"So who is that guy?" Nick asked. "Did he kidnap Winston?"

Addie shrugged. "Why would he want to?"

Mr. McCormick shook his head. "There doesn't seem to be a logical explanation for any of this. I think our best bet is to call the police and give them the information we have. They'll contact the authorities in New York. Maybe they can make some sense out of it."

Mr. Sutton agreed. "Let me get the chief of police on the telephone. I think he might respond a little ... better if we talk to him here."

Miss T. gave a short laugh. "You think he might not believe an old woman who walked into his station and told him she was Tierny Bryce?"

Mr. Sutton grinned. "He might be a tad ... skeptical."

Evidently the newspaper had a good working relationship with the police department, because it was only a matter of minutes before the chief of police walked into the newspaper office.

He was a tall man, with a quick smile and an outgoing manner. He was also a friend of Eunice Tisdale.

"Hello, Don," she said warmly. "So you're the new chief of police! What a surprise. But a nice one."

"Thank you, Eunice," he said, but his expression was troubled. "Is there a problem I can help you with?"

"There certainly is," she replied and nodded at Mr. Sutton.

"Chief Powell," he said, "we need you to make some connections for us with the New York Police Department, but first I'd like you to read this." He handed the officer Miss T.'s statement.

Chief Powell took the paper and sat down next to his elderly friend. "Any nosy kids snooping around your house lately?" he asked with a grin.

Miss T. rolled her eyes and inclined her head toward the three children around her chair.

Chief Powell only laughed and began reading the neatly printed paper.

"Don was ten years old when he and a friend heard my house was haunted. One night they tried to sneak in one of the windows on the first floor. Don's friend boosted him up to the window sill, but he slipped and fell and broke his arm. I had to get out of bed and take him to the doctor to have it set. We've been friends ever since."

Chief Powell gave the children a sheepish grin and returned to his reading. Soon his smile faded and he glanced quickly at Miss T., then back at the paper. When he finished reading, he swallowed hard and struggled for the right words.

"Eunice," he said, half-laughing, "I'm not sure what to say here."

"Chief Powell, I'm convinced her story is true," Mr. Sutton interrupted smoothly.

"Oh, I don't doubt it for a minute," Chief Powell agreed, still smiling. "I've known this lady for

35 years and she always manages to surprise me. Nooooo, I believe it, all right, but oh, boy." He sighed heavily. "Eunice, have you got proof? I mean, after all these years, do you have anything that proves you're—you're who you say you are? *Tierny Bryce?!*"

"She's got the statue," Addie said, and the chief glanced back at the paper in his hand.

"Well, I suppose that's proof," he said. "But I meant an I.D. of some sort. Anything like that?"

Miss T. shook her head.

"All right," he said. Then he frowned. "Wait a minute. Why do you need me? What am I supposed to do? Why don't you just call the TV station and put her on the news tonight?"

Mr. Sutton took the newspaper Miss T. still held and pointed to the article about Winston and his driver. Chief Powell nodded.

"I see. That does change things, doesn't it? You think Rinehart was kidnapped by someone interested in finding that statue?"

"Possibly," Mr. Sutton said.

"Don't forget to tell him about Kirby Roberts," Nick added.

Sutton nodded. "When Winston Rinehart was in town last week, he was tailed by a man named Kirby Roberts. Roberts claimed to be a reporter for this newspaper, but we have no one on staff by that name."

Chief Powell drummed his fingers on the desk in front of him and chewed his bottom lip for several moments. "So. You want me to call the NYPD and tell them Tierny Bryce has . . . turned herself in, so to speak, and has information that could be critical in the search for Winston Rinehart?"

Everyone nodded.

Chief Powell chuckled quietly to himself. "All right," he finally said. "Let's do it." He stood up. "But I need that statue. It's all I've got for proof." He looked Miss T. in the eye. "I'm trusting you on this one, Eunice."

Miss T. stood up as well and faced the man squarely. "Have I ever disappointed you, Don?"

He smiled. "Never. Let's go. I'll take you home and pick up the statue. Who else is riding with me?"

"We will!" Nick exclaimed, and Addie and Brian grinned.

"Uh," Mr. Sutton coughed. "Mind if I tag along?" he asked.

"Of course not," Miss T. said. "You've been extremely helpful. I appreciate your tolerance of an old woman."

It was dark when they left the newspaper building. The ride back to Miss T.'s passed too quickly for the children. None of them had been in a police car before and Chief Powell answered all their questions patiently. He even showed Brian how quickly the computer could identify a person and his criminal history by punching in Miss T.'s license plate number. Her name came on the screen within seconds and Chief Powell explained what all the different information meant.

"Lucky you," he said to Miss T. "No prior convictions. I'd hate to have to arrest Tierny Bryce!"

They pulled into Miss T.'s drive and the house appeared dark until they stopped by the back door.

The light over the kitchen sink glowed softly through the window.

"I don't remember leaving that light on," she frowned.

They all got out of their cars and Miss T. fumbled with the key to the house. She finally got inside and hung the key in its customary spot on the hook by the door. Everyone crowded into the kitchen.

Miss T. draped her coat over a chair. "Addie, would you go get the statue from the front room, please?"

Addie nodded and hurried down the hall. She crossed the room to the china closet and gasped with dismay. The glass door was slightly ajar and the statue was gone.

CHAPTER 18

More Unusual Guests!

Miss T sat at the kitchen table, facing Police Chief Powell and Mr. Sutton. She smiled grimly.

"I won't blame you if you choose not to believe my story now. I know it looks bad. But there is a statue, and I am telling the truth."

"Eunice, I don't doubt your story. Not for a minute," the police chief said kindly. "But at this point, I have nothing to take to the authorities in New York. I can still call and tell them what you've told me, but I'm not sure they'll take it seriously."

Mr. Sutton nodded. "I've seen police logs from the NYPD. Not a day goes by that someone doesn't walk in off the street claiming to be Abe Lincoln or Santa Claus. The list is endless. A phone call from an elderly woman claiming to be Tierny Bryce won't mean a thing to them. You've got to have proof."

"All right," the old woman said firmly. "We'll find proof. I don't know how, but we will."

"What about Jack Krueger?" Mr. McCormick said suddenly.

"Of course!" Miss T. said jubilantly. "Jack can vouch for me."

"Jack . . . ?" asked Mr. Sutton.

"Jack Krueger directed Winston and me in almost all of the movies we made together. He helped me leave Hollywood."

Chief Powell smiled. "He's our man! Let's contact him immediately. When he verifies your identity and your story, we'll call the NYPD and—"

A loud crash outside the back door interrupted the chief and everyone jumped.

"Stay here," he said quietly. He opened the door and walked silently down the steps, his hand on his holster. There was a brief, tense silence, and then a loud shout.

"Go on, you ornery varmints, get outta here! Go on, shoo!"

Nick, Addie, and Brian ran to the door and watched as Chief Powell chased the last raccoon into the woods behind Miss T.'s.

The officer grinned as he came back in the kitchen. "Those your pets, Eunice? I've never seen raccoons that bold. You been feeding them?"

Miss T. laughed. "Well, I admit I don't discourage them the way I should."

Everyone relaxed and Addie closed the door behind Chief Powell. She glanced out the window to the darkness beyond. The raccoons were gone, but there were shadows flickering in the dim light from the kitchen window. Addie knew they were shadows of the tree branches blowing in the wind, but she still shivered. Then one shadow seemed to move down the side wall of the old building and she stiffened.

"Chief . . . ?" she said softly. He joined her at the window and she gazed intently into the darkness. He followed her stare, but the shadow was gone.

"Never mind. I guess I'm just nervous," she said, somewhat embarrassed.

He smiled and winked at her and she felt better. Nick started making spooky sounds under his breath and Addie stuck her tongue out at him.

"Eunice, if you would, call Mr. Krueger and ask him to contact me at this number," the chief said. He handed Miss T. a business card. "After I verify his call, I'll set up a conference call with you and the NYPD. We'll tell them what you've told me. That should get the ball rolling."

Miss T. nodded. "Thank you so much, Don. I appreciate your confidence in me. I won't forget this."

Chief Powell raised his eyebrows. "Believe me, Eunice, neither will I. Neither will I." He studied the old woman for several seconds, a slight smile on his face. "Tierny Bryce. *Tierny Bryce!*" He began to laugh. "What a hoot this is going to be!"

"That's an understatement," Mr. Sutton said with a grin. "Chief, can I have a ride back to town? I think I'm going to write this one up myself. You will keep me posted?" he asked Miss T.

"Of course," she nodded.

The two men let themselves out the back door. Chief Powell was still chuckling.

"I'm glad someone thinks this is a hoot," Miss T. said grumpily.

Addie sighed. "I don't. Winston is missing and now the statue is gone."

"And there's not a whole lot we can do about it," Mr. McCormick added, glancing at his watch. "We'd better get home. It's almost six o'clock. Eunice, let us know what happens tonight. And if there's anything more I can do—"

Miss T. shook her head. "You've done enough, John." Then she snapped her fingers. "Well, there is one more thing," she admitted with a laugh. "I've given the children an old recliner to put in their room, but none of us can get it up the attic stairs. I walked around it all day, and I'd like to get it out of the way. Could you possibly . . . ?"

"Sure," Mr. McCormick said, flexing his muscles. "Lead me to it."

The recliner was in the next room. Addie's father picked up the heavy end of the chair, and Brian and Addie each took an arm. The children went first, backing slowly up the stairs, and they bumped their way to the attic, with frequent stops for rest.

At the top of the stairs, Addie set her side down and reached through the door to turn on the light. Then she crossed the attic and pushed open the secret panel. Reaching inside, she flicked that light on and screamed.

Mr. McCormick heaved the chair to one side and ran across the attic to Addie. But his young daughter had recovered from her shock and stepped inside the hidden room.

Winston Rinehart and his driver sat on the floor, back to back, bound and gagged. Addie was already at Winston's side, fumbling with the knot on the handkerchief stuffed in his mouth.

"Thank the Lord!" Mr. McCormick breathed, and set to work untieing the ropes that bound both men's hands together. Brian untied Winston's feet, then Mr. Riker's. Once the driver's hands were freed, he removed his own gag and struggled to his feet.

Mr. McCormick helped Winston stand and the old man collapsed gratefully in the rocking chair. He rubbed his wrists and sucked in deep breaths of air. No one spoke for several moments and Mr. Riker stood stiffly at his boss's side.

"Are you all right, sir?" he asked anxiously, rubbing his own wrists.

"Of course, Wes," the old man nodded. "You?"

"Fine, fine."

Mr. McCormick turned to Brian. "Son, go downstairs and tell Miss T . . . tell her we'll need some water and some hot coffee."

"But—"

"I'm sure we'll hear the whole story when these gentlemen are able to tell it." Mr. McCormick gave the boy a gentle push. "Go on. We'll be right behind you."

Brian nodded and left the room. Addie could hear his soft footsteps padding down two flights of stairs and into the kitchen. Then the indistinct murmur of several voices talking at once could be heard and finally a very loud, very clear, *"What?"*

More footsteps pounded back up the stairs and this time Nick burst into the secret room. Surprise and relief flooded over his face when he saw Winston Rinehart. Brian was right behind him, grinning hugely.

"How in the world—"

"Not now Nick," Mr. McCormick said firmly. "We're getting these men downstairs before we do anything else."

Together they made their way back to the kitchen. Everyone, including Mr. Riker, hovered around

Winston until the old man laughed and waved them all away.

"Give me some room, or I'll fall down these stairs," he joked.

Miss T. was waiting at the door in the kitchen. Tears of joy came to her eyes when she saw her old friend, and they embraced tightly.

"Here, sit down, Winston, before you fall down," the old woman commanded gruffly. She helped him to a chair at the table.

"I'm so sorry, Tee," Mr. Rinehart murmured. "I'm so sorry."

"Whatever for?" Miss T. demanded.

"I'm afraid the news is out."

"I *know* the news is out," she replied. "I put it out myself. Went to the newspaper and the police. They've got the whole story."

"But why?"

"The police might have connected your disappearance to your problems with Conrad Carter and the statue, but only I knew where the statue was. I couldn't keep that information to myself, not when you were in danger."

Mr. Rinehart lifted Miss T.'s hand to his lips and kissed it gently. "Thank you, my dear," he said. "About the statue . . ."

"The statue is gone," Addie informed him.

Winston shook his head. "Kirby Roberts has it."

"That nasty reporter," fumed Mr. Riker, "who really isn't a reporter at all."

"It's really very simple," Mr. Rinehart sighed. "Kirby Roberts III is the grandson, and namesake, of Kirby Roberts.

"Kirby Roberts," Addie said slowly. "K R—the initials on the bottom of the statue!"

"Exactly," said Mr. Rinehart and he began his story. "Kirby Roberts was a student of Conrad Carter. We thought Carter sculpted all the statues for the movie, but we were wrong. Carter tutored Kirby in the art of sculpting and the student soon surpassed the teacher. Many of the sculptures used in *Spies for Sale* were the creation of Mr. Kirby. Carter took credit for them, of course.

"On one of the sculptures, though, Kirby managed to engrave his initials in a location that went unnoticed until after the movie was made. When Carter discovered what Kirby had done, he was furious.

"He tried to recover the statue before anyone would find out his student was the real artist. But Tee had disappeared by then, and so had the statue.

"Carter lived in fear that the truth would be revealed and his reputation ruined. And Kirby had no proof that the statues were his creation. He died a bitter old man, but not before he passed on his bitterness to his son—and his grandson."

"*Our* Kirby Roberts," Addie said.

The old man nodded. "When the grandson heard I had acquired many of Tierny Bryce's mementos, he went to the museum to find the statue. It wasn't there, of course, so he began tailing me.

"I suppose I should have been more secretive in my contacts with you, Tee, but I honestly didn't think anyone would ever follow me. It didn't take the young man long to trace me back to this house. When he did, he knew he was on to something.

"So he followed Wes and I to the car rental shop Sunday morning. He was still posing as a reporter then and offered us a ride to the airport in exchange for some answers to a few questions.

"I thought I would humor the young man. That was my mistake. Mr. Kirby took us, at gunpoint, to an abandoned house only a few miles from here."

"So how did you end up in my attic?" Miss T. demanded.

Winston shook his head. "I can't really explain that one myself. Roberts somehow got a key to your home, and just an hour or so ago he took us directly to the room in the attic. How he got the key and how he knew about that room is a mystery to me."

Just then the reflected glare of headlights bounced off the kitchen wall and everyone watched a police car pull slowly down the drive. Chief Powell stepped out of the car and strode purposefully up the back steps. Miss T. met him at the door and had it open before he even knocked.

"Tierny Bryce, I presume?" he asked with a mischievous grin. "I believe this belongs to you." The missing statue was cradled in his hands.

"I'm Ready"

"It seems everything's turning up in strange places tonight," Miss T. said with some amusement.

Chief Powell smiled. "I happened to run into Kirby Roberts a few minutes ago, so I relieved him of this statue." He nodded at Winston Rinehart and Mr. Riker. "I'm glad to see you gentlemen are all right. When Kirby told me where you were, I came back to make sure someone had found you. And I wanted Eunice to know her statue had been found. But I'm afraid I have to take it in to the station now for evidence."

"What kind of evidence?" Mr. McCormick asked.

"Evidence to charge Kirby Roberts with theft. And that's just for starters."

Mr. McCormick was still confused. "Where'd you find Roberts?"

"I decided to check out the country roads in the area, just to see if there was any unusual activity. I knew Eunice was telling the truth about her statue. I thought maybe the thief was still in the area."

"So there *was* someone by the greenhouse tonight," Addie said triumphantly. "I knew I wasn't seeing things."

Chief Powell nodded. "After Kirby locked Mr. Rinehart and Mr. Riker in the attic, he hung around

until Eunice got home. He wanted to be sure someone would be here to find the two men. I found his
car on the road that borders the wooded side of your
property, Eunice. I parked about a quarter mile
away and waited. It was only a few minutes before
he came out of those woods—with the statue."

Nick was puzzled. "I still don't understand how
Kirby Roberts got into your house, Miss T."

"I don't either," she replied.

"Evidently he came to visit you yesterday and
got . . . sidetracked by Amy," Chief Powell said.
Addie stifled a giggle at the memory, and even Miss
T. smiled at the chief's tactful interpretation of the
previous day's events.

"Instead of leaving, he merely got in his car and
pulled out of the drive. Then he came back to the
kitchen, saw Amy had left, and heard voices upstairs. He sneaked up to the attic, but you all were
enjoying yourselves so much you didn't hear him.

"When he saw the secret room, he knew he'd
found an answer to his main problem—what to do
with his 'prisoners.' So he left again, but not before
he'd taken the spare key you leave hanging on a
hook by your back door." Chief Powell cocked an
eyebrow at the old woman and she frowned.

"Oh, don't look at me like that. My keys have
hung there for the last 45 years and no one ever stole
them before."

"Where's Kirby now?" Addie asked.

"In the car, handcuffed to the door. Mr. Sutton is
watching him until I get back out there. Then Sutton would like to stay here, if you don't mind,
Eunice, and ask you some questions. He wants to

break the story in tomorrow morning's edition of the *Daily Gazette*."

The old woman sat up straight and took a deep breath. "So now it starts," she said softly. Amy reached out and rested her hand lightly on the woman's shoulder.

Miss T. looked around at the roomful of faces. Winston smiled tenderly at his old friend. Mr. McCormick winked. Brian and Nick both grinned and Nick gave her the thumbs up sign. Addie blinked hard, but managed to smile and reach out to take Miss T.'s hand.

"When I left Hollywood 45 years ago, I didn't have anyone. Now I have all of you. And in the few months I've known you, you've always been there for me."

"And we always will be," Addie said softly.

Miss T. squeezed the young girl's hand. "I know, dear, I know." She looked at Chief Powell and smiled. "I'm ready," she said.

Don't Miss Any of Addie McCormick's Exciting Adventures!

———

Addie McCormick and the Stranger in the Attic

A vanishing visitor and secrets from the past... can Addie and Nick put the puzzle together before something terrible happens to their friend Miss T.?

Addie McCormick and the Mystery of the Missing Scrapbook

A missing scrapbook, mysterious paintings, and an old letter lead Nick, Addie, and Brian on a heartstopping chase. Are they in over their heads this time?

Addie McCormick and the Stolen Statue

A movie star has been kidnapped and Miss T.'s statue has disappeared! Facing their toughest mystery yet, Addie, Nick, and Brian have all the clues... but can they put them together before it's too late?

Addie McCormick and the Chicago Surprise

When things start disappearing from their hotel room in Chicago, Addie and Nick are determined to solve the mystery. But what they discover about the thief is much more than they bargained for!